THE
PLEASURE
YOU SUFFER
A SAUDADE
ANTHOLOGY

THE PLEASURE YOU SUFFER

A SAUDADE ANTHOLOGY

Edited By Gerald Brennan and Leanna Gruhn

Tortoise Books
Chicago, IL

FIRST EDITION, JUNE, 2016

Table of Contents

saudade

(n.) (in Portuguese or Brazilian folklore) a feeling of longing, melancholy, or nostalgia for someone or something that is absent; "the love that remains"

[My] Memories of [Your] Sex Life

Lily Mooney

You go to high school in rural New England. We haven't met. You suffer under a blanket of acne, struggle constantly to hide sudden, irrepressible erections, and skip lunch most days. You lust after a blonde, hourglassy girl named Lindsay who sings in choir, and the musicals, and wants to be an actress. I don't know for sure that you masturbate to her, but you probably masturbate to her. I don't know how you masturbate, but you share a bedroom with your grandmother, so I imagine, whether to Lindsay or to Natalie Portman, it's quiet.

....

You are a freshman in college in upstate New York. We've met once in passing; we dismissed each other. You're majoring in English and learning Japanese. You lust after a girl on your floor named Ari—the tall, gorgeous, half-Japanese daughter of New York socialites. She likes you because you're funny, and charmingly poor, and a non-threatening source of male attention. You jerk off nightly to thoughts of her, and in a year you'll jerk off to the selfies she posts on the growing social networking website, thefacebook.com. Your roommate is now a guy your own age, so I imagine from time to time you allow yourself a few audible moans.

....

At the end of junior year, before you leave for the summer, you convince me to drive you to an off-campus Wendy's. Returning to school, we park by the woods and talk. I watch you devour two double cheeseburgers, a large milkshake, and fries; the grease gleams darkly on your lips as tiny bun-seeds fall onto your lap, and my floor.

....

In the fall of senior year a dark-haired, doe-eyed junior starts sitting beside us in our documentary film course. She makes idle conversation before class, directed at you. Convinced that attractive women have no interest in you, you initially mistrust the signals she sends.

A month later, you lose your virginity in her dorm room after a failed attempt where your nerves make it impossible for you to get hard. She's patient—persistent—and after abandoning all hope, suddenly you are hard, and you fuck her with a mixture of triumph and terror, screaming primally for her roommates to hear. You fuck like rabbits every day until she leaves in February to study abroad in New Zealand.

....

In the spring, I confess my feelings for you, to you, weeks before we graduate. We're in your dorm room after you convinced me to drive you to Stop & Shop so that you could, inexplicably, buy 4 separate gallon-jugs of distilled water. You tell me you love me like a sister, and I leave.

The night before graduation, you meet a girl whose name you'll forget. She hangs around until everyone else falls asleep and slithers into your bedroom. You go down on each other until sunrise, when she leaves to get her cap & gown. You struggle through the inspirational speeches, raccoon-eyed, and look for her afterward, but never see her again. Was her name Dana?

....

A year later, you and I road trip to Chicago to find an apartment. We both want to relocate, and decide to share a place. You invite your best friend from childhood; his aunt lives in Chicago and will let us stay in her basement. For fun, I invite my childhood best friend, and the four of us laugh and joke through the sixteen-hour drive to the Midwestern city that will soon be our home. The first night, after your best friend and I drift off, you and my best friend strip naked and hook up for hours on the red leather couch in the humid basement den where we're crashing. You receive a long, slow blowjob from my childhood best friend on that couch, five feet from me, dozing on the floor in a sleeping bag. Your best friend seems to be asleep, but he isn't. He's five feet away on the other side of you, awake with his eyes closed, breathing and listening.

....

One summer evening, you and I find ourselves alone in New York City with heavy backpacks and no place to spend the night. I suggest we wander outside till sunrise, but you want to be indoors. We argue. You convince me to split a hotel room. In this era before smartphones, we rely on directions from strangers, and we land in an expensive room with one bed on the smoking floor of a hotel with a nightclub in the lobby. A month before this night, I broke up with my boyfriend of nearly three years. You've been single since that girl went to New Zealand, with just one blowjob in all that time, received in Chicago, from my childhood best friend, on the red leather couch. At 3 AM we lie in bed next to each other, not talking, and not touching.

....

You and I move into separate apartments, and you start reading *The House of Leaves*. Your roommate read it last year, and tried to get you to read it; you refused, and made fun of it for the better part of a year. Now you're reading *The House of Leaves*. A girl at work named Samantha lent it to you. Samantha comes over one night, and the two of you dry hump on the living room sofa until you cum inside your cargo shorts. She gets a cab home. Meanwhile, your roommate rereads *The House of Leaves* in his room.

....

Arriving together in Boston to visit our families, my parents ask me to meet them at an animal hospital where they are waiting to put down our family dog. You stand next to me as I put a hand on Buster's side. His chest heaves as he lies on the metal table. We exit together so they can give him the injection. You walk with me out of the hospital as my parents leave in their car.

....

A married woman is with you, in your bedroom, ripping off your clothes. After pursuing you for weeks at work, online, and at a party earlier this evening, she's caught you. The two of you make out sitting together on a toilet and then stumble into a cab. Now hidden in your apartment, with your roommate snoring across the hall, you realize that guilt can be a potent aphrodisiac. The married woman pushes you onto your bed and mounts you like a male lion.

....

You move into an overpriced one-bedroom apartment in Logan Square. I'm between apartments and jobs, and you let me stay for a week on your floor. Every morning before work you make us breakfast. Every night we stay in and talk. On the last night we stand in your closet and I dress you for a friend's party, convincing you to go so you can talk to girls, because you've spent the last several months, or years, alone.

At the party, one of the host's roommates likes your jokes and follows you from room to room. She invites you to sleep on the couch after it gets late. Possessed by an unfamiliar confidence, you talk your way from the couch to her bed, where she jerks you off with her hands. After you finish, when you search for your cum on the sheets, or your pants, or her pants, she holds up two dry palms and says "Magic Hands," then turns over and falls immediately asleep.

You arrive home the next day to find me sitting outside your door. I left in the morning and locked myself out. I'd called your phone, with no answer. I wandered your streets looking for something to do. I returned to your stoop, and I sat. I waited.

....

You court and then date a redhead who works in a cubicle ten feet to your left and lives with her parents in the suburbs. You take her to a magic show. She takes you to *Christkindlmart.* You start to spend weekends in the suburbs. Despite Herculean efforts, you are unable to give her an orgasm, although every time after you finish, when you ask her to, she will lie on her stomach facing away from you and get herself off. After eight months of this, you break up with her—your first time breaking up with anybody. Neither of you said "I love you," not even once.

....

Saudade

You start to lust after your coworkers in threes. Up to now, there was always the one curvy registrar, the one exotic receptionist, the shy accounting assistant, the bookish copywriter, that one woman who made long days in a corporate office bearable and lulled you to sleep at night. But now it's trios of women: the three women in sales, who sit with you at lunch; the brunette, blonde and redhead on your team, who like to take you shopping at an outlet mall. As months pass and you plunge into a sexless depression, your female co-workers are always there for you, in your fantasies. You live alone now, finally, and when you masturbate each night, you don't moan, or softly grunt. You sing. You wail. You keen.

....

You sit in my apartment for an entire afternoon, shooing my cat off your lap and yelling at me. It's sleeting in the evening as I walk you to the train station after convincing you not to talk to me anymore. When we hug goodbye, you lock your elbows at your sides and embrace me with tiny T-rex arms, ensuring space between us. You ask if I think we will ever be friends again. I say I don't know, but I hope.

After we stop talking, you see a therapist, join a gym, start a workout routine, lose 20 pounds, take a swing dancing class, take a playwriting class, and learn to cook. You go on blind dates and OkCupid dates and have three fiery one night stands before meeting Sarah, a smart, passionate union organizer who you date casually, and then seriously. You fuck Sarah on Fridays, after your work weeks are finished, usually after going on a date. You try things in bed from time to time. You keep things nice, the relationship is nice. It's manageable. It's grown-up. The sex is good.

....

You and Sarah break up amicably after almost a year of being together. You break up because you have decided to move to the West Coast and neither of you wants a long-distance thing. After a month of feeling down and preparing for your move, you perform stand-up one night at an open mic downtown. There you meet a woman who gets your number, takes you to lunch, and then pulls you back to your place, where she fucks you athletically all afternoon and evening. When you go out of town that week to visit your mother, she sexts you the entire time, which begins with dirty language and escalates into a series of pornographic picture-texts unlike any you have ever received. When you get back, you end it to avoid getting more attached, but not before one final exhausting night with her.

....

A week before you move, you and I rent a car and make a long drive to South Carolina to attend a mutual friend's wedding. On the way we joke and play-fight. In ten years of knowing each other, we are as close as we've ever been. At 2AM, we stop at a crusty Red Roof Inn in Tennessee before driving the final few hours to Asheville in the morning. Although you reserved a room with two beds, we arrived so late that they have to put us on a king-size. As we follow a bleary-eyed attendant to our room, making jokes about how grimy the bed will surely be, you look at me and blurt, "If you try to touch my dick, I will *freak out.*"

The attendant unlocks our door. We wash up and go to sleep. In the morning we put on our nice clothes, changing in the bathroom one after the other. We have a great time at the wedding.

....

The night before you move, I arrive at your studio apartment, where you've lived the past two years, to help you clean and pack your things into your car. Your apartment is empty of furniture and there are large amounts of trash organized in piles all over your floor. You talk to yourself and pace between the piles in your underwear, reeking of breakdown. I help you throw your things away. We vacuum, sweep, scrub, and Febreze. We're sweaty and you're calmer when we close your door for the last time. We get in your new car, your first car, bought last week for the move and now packed to the gills. We drive to my apartment, where you'll sleep in this city one final time—in my bed.

....

In the morning we stand by your car and we cry. We hold each other tight in a hug. You say I'm the most interesting person you've ever met. I can feel the entire length of your torso pressed against mine: your chest hair, your heartbeat. It's over now.

Saudade

We pull apart quick, like lids around an eye. You walk away, and drive away. The space between us grows. It's not empty, or sad. It's rich. It's the source—the definition—of sight; of clarity; of *alert*; of *awake.*

Gasoline Rainbow

Alfonso Mangione

WHAT IS IT that I fear

Falling asleep or waking up?

Drop a coin into my cup

And I'll tell you what you want to hear;

I'll beg you

And I'll bless you and thank you

And you can tell me what to do,

You seem to know more than I do

What do you know? My leg's swollen in this
dirty tennis shoe,

Skin like a drum, tight, so maybe I want the
night

Falling from a great height to a great sleep
might

Hurt more than this, but only for an instant

Then…bliss?

Who knows, first

Bones will crack, vessels burst,

Blood spread across the sidewalk—

I see it in the worst way

Too clearly, replay it too frequently

Maybe I gotta do it just to stop the imagery?

How come I don't? Am I just cowardly?

Still sleep itself seems easy,

Actions without consequences

In my dreams nonsensical,

And I can leave the theater

And talk about these movies to people who'll never see them

But are they only entertaining

When I'm explaining them to you

On a new morning

Under the awning

Outside the White Hen when it's raining?

I say I can't complain but I'm complaining

I want dreams all year long, not just summer
When I slumber on an island of grass
With taxis and cops circling like sharks, they don't stop,
Just go elsewhere so I can relax and not react
Unlike winter when night's like day
Bright and angry on the CTA
Pockets picked near vomit smell
In that rocking fluorescent motel
Electric hell;
But the summer nights are easy
Black like me and blue and cool too,
A sleazy pleasant lover,
While day's always a nagging wife
Unfortunately not an option unless I opt for endless night
To escape that demanding bitch, I used to auction off my time to her

So I could afford to spend it all on the other
Until she took over
Was that my choice?
Still I didn't mind,
I might have decided not to fight
But I thought there were no consequences
To night, just dreams, and spills to clean up with repentances
Still, escapes from our life sentences
With the eternal wife, our ball and chain
Old dull routine
Clanging alarms and cramped commutes,
Working for bosses with golden parachutes
While my only options were worthless
Somewhere between toilet paper and vapor
I needed a few toots to escape, or—
What? That's all it was, a different road
Than the one you took to the bar
Dirty rocks or maybe black tar

Which made me feel far from harm

At last! Safe in a warm hug, a liquid blanket

So snug it fit inside me.

Nod out, or take the other which would shake me up

Or powder my nose to wake me up

A white drug, but I liked it sometimes, I could make me up

Like I was Superman,

Or later just Clark Kent

When I felt bent out of shape, from partying away the rent

I could at least transform into a normal human being

A superhero feat I can't pull off now

Without at least a cheap disguise,

Hat or sunglasses to cover my eyes,

(Bloodshot or dilated or in between highs)

And hide the lies I tell to you to escape the lows.

Still everybody knows but you, or do you, too?

What does it matter if I get a fatter

Wad of bills to pay the boss?

You can treat me with utter contempt, it's no loss,

Just don't tempt me

Into acting the fool

When you butter my bread, I can't afford that

So I'll give you more of that wicked flow,

I'm a gasoline rainbow

Drifting past you in the gutter

Greasy, easy

Lazy, slow

I don't know what I done wrote,

Is it a poem or a suicide note?

Who knows?

These flows are the only

Way out of my lonely

(Unless no one's really listening,

And I'm howling into the void

Annoyed

As I drift towards that gaping hole

Do you feel me? How can you, you're employed,

Still maybe you fear the night, too)

But do I really want a new day

Or a way out of this fear?

Who can say?

Drop a coin into my cup

And I'll tell you what you want to hear—

Out of the Blue

Jennifer Schaefer

1996

In her knee-high stiletto boots, she steps outside and regards the swollen monochrome sky. Great. More effing rain. Vulturine pigeons watch from rafters, poised to swoop for scraps scattered by the human stampede below, foreigners and Londoners alike, marching rapidly, purposefully, endlessly through the rank Soho streets. Techno music throbs from murky doorways and neon signs pulse their ware: LATE NITE COCKTAILS, SUPER MAGS, CHINESE TAKEAWAY and GIRLS GIRLS GIRLS.

Ducking under an awning, she fondles the contraband in her jacket pocket and scans the streets for a cab. Screw it, she finally decides, bolting into the downpour. Better just grab a bus at Piccadilly.

All she wants is to go home; home to her lovely flat on the Thames. But she promised herself she'd do it after the audition today; she'd finally stick to her guns and do it.

Normally, she loves the bus, loves to find a seat on top to survey the city. *Her* city. For the double-decker bus is hers. That Tower Records right there is hers. The ghostly Houses of Parliament, blazing like copper flames in the inky dark, hers. The River Thames, hers. That trendy shop with the clueless sales assistants, useless alarm system and clothes that slip oh-so-easily into her handbag, hers. That nightclub, newsagent's, tasty spiky-haired guy chasing after the bus. Hers, hers and all hers.

"Excuse me," says someone, tapping her shoulder. Two teenage girls in the seat behind her. "Aren't you the one in the whatsit advert?"

"Selfridges," she nods, then laughs. "No autographs, please."

The girls chirp something to one another; she turns back to the rain-glittered window. Though she'd left Wisconsin almost a year ago, it's still so surreal, her new life.

Anyway. Pissing rain or not, she's finally going to do it. Now. Finally, for the first time, she's going to meet her mother.

Narcotic courage, she thinks, fishing the pill from her pocket.

....

1987

It had started with a rock. Eighth grade. *Thud.* Inches from her head. *Thunk.* Another, this one ricocheting off her gym shoe. She lifted her eyes to the cluster of smirking girls. Kelly Rasmussen's grin glinted like a razor as she hurled another rock.

But then: the bleating bell. Recess was over.

No big deal. She'd just keep her distance and they'd lose interest. But things just got worse. Would they push in front of her at the drinking fountain? Mock her facial tic? Tease her about her alkie dad and absent mother?

Every day her cheek twitching, stomach in knots until the blessed dismissal bell.

....

On the woody embankment behind her house, she removed the joint and lighter from her pocket. Quick—before she chickened out. But taking the hit, she doubled over coughing.

"Aren't you a little young for that?"

Her head snapped up. A teenage boy on the path. A couple years older, sixteen or so. White-blonde hair, golden skin. Glowing like an angel in his stonewashed jeans and starched tee.

"Where'd you get that stuff?" he asked.

"My dad."

"No joke? Well, what would your old man think about you raiding his stash?" When she didn't reply, he chuckled. "Where is he anyway?"

"Some bar."

"What about your mom?"

She dropped her gaze. "In England, I guess. Where she's from."

He gestured to her oversized Bob Marley T-shirt. "Is your dad a hippie?"

"I guess."

"Good for him. Didn't figure there'd be any in this sorry-ass cheesehead town. So you like living in Lake Geneva?"

"Not really. Where are you from?"

"Cali. I'm just here for a couple days visiting my grandma." He extracted a pack of Marlboro Lights from his pocket. "Trade ya?"

"Okay," she said, exchanging smokes.

"Don't take such a huge hit this time." He demonstrated with the joint. "Good. Now give the J another shot," he said, handing it back to her. "Try to hold it in this time. Atta girl."

All she could do was smile. How tingly she felt! And how luminous his skin and hair against the velvety sky.

Abruptly, he snatched the joint from her lips and pinched it out. "Will your old man notice this is missing?" When she shook her head, he pocketed the joint. "Bummer. I'm leaving day after tomorrow."

"Where are you going?"

"Back to LA."

"Oh."

"Unless you're free tomorrow? Say around five?"

"I don't know," she said, casting a quick look over her shoulder. "Depends on if my dad..."

But the boy had vanished.

....

Counting the hours till five the next

day. Would he be there? Would he maybe try to kiss her? Just in case, she applied some cherry lip balm and affixed her new gold hoop earrings (hopefully unmissed by her dad's latest one-night stand). Don't get your hopes up, she told herself as she left the house. But when she climbed the embankment, there he was in his same chalk-white clothes, shouldering a backpack. "Hi," she smiled.

"Hi yourself." He set off down the path, towards the old train bridge.

So she trailed him over the bridge, down the muddy slope and onto the huge concrete drainpipe that ran under the bridge above a rushing stream. Without a word, they sat side by side on the pipe, backs pressed against the icy bridge wall.

Opening his backpack, he pulled out two wads of napkin. "Courtesy of my grandma."

She unfolded her napkin. "Brownies?"

"Not just any brownies. When Gran wasn't looking, I snuck in the rest of your dad's pot."

"Oh. Cool."

After polishing off his brownie, the boy nodded at her baggy Neil Young top. "Daddy's T-shirt again, huh? Your old man's got good taste in music." He cocked his head at her. "Man, are you gonna be gorgeous someday...when you...fill out and stuff. You've seriously gotta look me up then." Removing a pen from his backpack, he scrawled a phone number onto her napkin. "Give me a call someday, hear?" Then he reached into his backpack again. A camera. "I was thinking I could maybe take a few pictures? To remember you by?"

"Um. I guess so."

"Great. It's too bright out here though. Come on." Standing, he led her up the embankment again, but headed in the opposite direction, away from her house. Stepping off the path, he trampled downhill towards a garage at the bottom.

She stopped dead. "This is Kelly Rasmussen's yard."

But he just opened the side garage door and strode right in. "Out of the blue," he nodded at her T-shirt as she followed, "and into the black."

Inside: the usual summery reek of gasoline and tires, jumble of bikes and boxes. Plus a sheet stretched across the wall like a white backdrop. "Could you stand over there?" he said, training his camera on the sheet. "And maybe pull your shirt off one shoulder a little?"

She shivered as the garage door slammed shut.

....

Why was everyone gathered at her locker laughing? There was something taped to it, she saw as she approached. A photo of her sprawled across the oily garage floor in just her bra and shorts. When she finally got her locker open, out rained more photos.

Kelly Rasmussen gave a shriek. "Is that *my* garage?"

"Slut," said another girl, scooping up a photo. "Freak."

In the girls' restroom, she shut herself in a cubicle and flushed the napkin with his number down the toilet.

....

1993

Visiting her in Madison five years later, her father paused outside Pipefitters on State Street. "A head shop. That brings me back."

She sighed. "We can go in if you want."

"Nah, I've given up the stuff. Come on, let's grab some lunch." But then he stopped again, this time to watch some dreadlocked street musician warbling Grateful Dead songs.

"Come *on*." She nudged him along. "I'm *starving*."

"Nothing beats campus life," he smiled, tossing a dollar into the open guitar case.

Inside oaky Amy's Cafe, her dad did most of the talking, reminiscing about his college days.

"Until I came along." She stole a sip of his beer. "And cramped your style."

"Aw, hon. I didn't mean that."

A gangly pin-headed man with slicked-back hair burst into the cafe and started stacking chairs onto tables. "Time to go! Go home, poseurs!"

But everyone stayed put: it was just Kozmo.

"Not closing time, Koz," said a waiter. "Come back at two *a.m.*, man."

Kozmo's mouth puckered. "Hey, what's that smell? It's sick!"

"Dunno, Koz," said the waiter, restoring the upturned chairs to the floor.

"It's probably that dragon I slew in the basement! Haven't you guys cleaned it up yet?"

"Must've slipped my mind. Come back in twelve hours, okay, Koz?"

Kozmo, on his way out the door, took in her lacey blouse and tartan skirt. "You look real nice, baby. There should be a dress code in these places, you hear me? When I'm mayor things are gonna change around here!"

"What's with that guy, anyway?" asked her dad.

"Oh, he's harmless. He's actually okay if you catch him in a lucid mood. And apparently very effective at clearing out the drunks at closing time. He comes into Ragstock,   too."

"Speaking of," said her dad, glancing

at his watch. "Shouldn't you be getting back to work, kiddo?"

....

Ironically, she'd gotten her job while nabbing items for her wardrobe. Ragstock was a shoplifter's dream. A cinch to grab a bunch of clothes, duck into a dressing room, slip half the stuff on under her own clothes, then emerge nonchalantly with the other unwanted items afterwards. Indeed, it was while doing so that she'd seen the HELP WANTED note taped to the mirror. She'd applied for the position wearing two layers of lifted clothes beneath her own.

....

She'd first seen Kozmo a couple years before; he'd marched into Steep-n-Brew coffeehouse wearing a bell-bottomed denim jumpsuit and lugging a boom box. She'd watched, curious, as he plugged it in, pressed Play, and cranked the volume: Black Sabbath.

"Right on," she laughed above the din as he strummed an air guitar.

"I AM IRON MAN!" he replied, high-fiving her.

Until an employee unplugged the boom box. "You know it's not open-mike tonight, Koz."

"Get off my fucking oasis," sulked Kozmo. Then he waved the cafe guy away and nodded at the roomful of students nose-deep in textbooks. "Most of these people don't even try anymore. They just gave up. You hear me? You hear me, don't ya? BAH-HA-HA!"

....

Though she'd quit college, she was still a regular at the local cafes and clubs. Other than Kozmo, people rarely spoke to her. Until one night a bartender handed her a business card: "Friend of mine works for Bacardi and is looking for a hot girl for some kind of promotions gig."

At first, the job seemed easy enough; all she had to do was go bar-hopping with two guys, the slick Bacardi rep and the beefcake male model. The first stop was some sports bar, where she found herself in a Bacardi Babe tank top and tight shorts, circling the bar with a tray of shots.

When they'd run through all the rum, it was game time, which basically involved hurling logo hats and T-shirts into the drunken crowd. The crowning glory, though, was the photo shoot: she'd stand against a tropical backdrop as the rep collected money from guys wishing to pose for Polaroids with the Bacardi Babe.

SLUT, rang the adolescent voices in her ear as the camera flashed. FREAK.

"Are you okay?" asked the rep, when she recoiled from the guy who'd paid to stand beside her. "Loosen up. Have a shot."

She did.

"Holy crap!" she cried later: two hundred dollars in tips. Not such a bad racket, all in all.

....

One day while she was folding T-shirts at Ragstock, Kozmo came in and placed a huge straw sombrero on his head. "You know Kozmo's just an alias, right? My real name is Bob. Rock and Roll Bob. My sisters used to call me Blobster. I was a really fat kid. Can you believe it? BAH-HA-HA!"

"Oh, you have sisters?"

"Two. And a brother in the CIA. I live with my mom. I won't live in any of the dives my case worker keeps showing me. It's hard to find a good apartment these days. This town's been taken over by villains. Don't blow my cover, okay doll-face?"

"I won't, don't worry. Well, I gotta get back to work."

"Be careful, hear me? They've got this place bugged. This place is full of spies."

"Spies?"

"There's more international espionage going on in Madtown than anywhere else in the world." He placed the sombrero on her head. "So stop stealing, you hear me? Or you'll be in too deep and I won't be able to help you. You hear me, don't you?"

....

After a Bacardi job one night, she made the mistake of turning down her usual ride home from the rep.

"Hey, Bacardi Babe! Wait up!"

Shit, some drunk guy from the bar.

"Hey," he said, at her side now. "Where are you going? To your boyfriend's?"

"Maybe."

"You're lying. You're different, I can tell. I'm different too."

"Yeah? How so?"

"I'm the oldest guy in my frat. I'm twenty-six."

"You sure you want to admit that?"

"Hey, I was in the Marines after high school. Keeping *your* ass safe and free. Wanna go for a drink?"

"You've probably had enough, don't you think?"

"Where do you live? I'll walk you home."

"I don't think my boyfriend would be cool with that."

"Well, what would your boyfriend say about this?" In a mechanical motion, he grabbed her face and stuck his tongue in her mouth.

"Gee, that was romantic," she said mildly, moving away.

"That's just the way I operate."

"Well," she said, turning away. "Bye."

He blocked her path. "You're asking to get raped, you know that? Walking around dressed like that."

She froze, cheek twitching, heart hammering.

And then, a movement in the distance caught her eye—some large-headed form with wings careening towards them. Kozmo. On his bicycle. In a flapping, unbuttoned Hawaiian shirt and sombrero, no less.

And then here he was, circling them on his silver BMX. "Hi, pumpkin. How are you?"

"She's fine," said the frat guy. "Take a hike."

She caught Kozmo's eye. "No. Don't."

Kozmo leapt off his bike. "What's the matter, doll-face?"

The guy hesitated, then turned tail. "Freak," he spat, stumbling off.

And she realized at last that she'd been holding her breath, clenching her hands. She relaxed, just a little.

"Overrun with kooks, this town," Kozmo said. "BAH-HA-HA!"

"Well, I should be getting home."

"This isn't your home, doll-face."

"What do you mean? Sure, it is."

"Oh, yeah? Well, if this is your home, where's your mommy? You hear me? I know you fucking hear me."

She turned and walked away.

....

Well, Madison was certainly more her home than Lake Geneva these days. So depressing, how rundown her dad was looking. From all the beer and pot? Hopefully nothing harder. It was this concern that sent her snooping through his room Christmas morning. But what she uncovered in his dresser drawer was almost more unsettling: a stack of *Penthouse* pay stubs.

She cornered him in the kitchen. "Let me guess. You lead a secret double life as a sleazy photographer?"

He glanced at the pay stubs she'd dumped on the table. "Don't I wish."

"Gross. Those girls are, like, my age."

He mimicked her sour face. "Lighten up, kiddo."

"So what's the deal? Do you sell subscriptions or something?"

"No," he said with a sheepish grin. "I just do a little, shall we say…creative writing for them sometimes."

"I don't get it."

"They have a section, you know, a readers' letters kind of thing. It's just to make a little extra money."

With a noise of disgust, she ran to her bedroom and slammed the door. What kind of dad spent all his free time in bars? Brought home a different woman every night? Earned money by writing porn?

"If this is your home," blared Kozmo's voice in her skull, "where's your mommy?"

....

Wandering up State Street several weeks later, she happened upon Kozmo sprawled on a bench bashing away on a half-strung guitar.

"What's up, Koz? I haven't seen you in forever."

"I've been on a bat-hunting expedition in Bohemia."

"Sounds exciting."

"Exciting? It was terrible. Bats are sick! Vermin!" Then he sprung off down the street.

"Where are you going? Don't forget your guitar."

"Leave it there. No one dares meddle with Rock and Roll Bob's magic machinery."

After she'd caught up with him, he stage-whispered: "Coffee's the only safe sustenance. I can't eat anything at home. My food is being poisoned." Outside a gyros place, he paused to watch a gory slab of meat being carved in the window.

"Can I buy you something to eat, Koz?"

"I hate Greek food! Aristotle was a jerk!"

"Well, let's get some coffee at least."

In the tweedy fug of Steep-n-Brew, she raised her mug. "Here's to you, Bob."

"I told you not to blow my cover, remember? It's crucial to your safety and mine that as far as everyone's concerned, I'm just crazy Kozmo."

"Sorry. I forgot."

He pointed to his pimply forehead. "And these aren't zits! They're bullet holes!"

"Wow. Those must hurt like hell."

"You're such a honey. Wanna come back to my place and tend to my wounds? I won't let you give me my medication though." Then he leapt from the table. "Let's blow this popsicle stand, pumpkin-face. There's something I need to tell you. In private."

Outside, she had to jog to match his spidery gait as he launched off across Library Mall, up steep Bascom Hill.

"Hey, where are we going, Koz?"

"Three hundred years ago the Indians ran up and down this hill fifty times a day! Squaws too! The Indians were in great fucking shape! Didn't even stop to scratch their balls! I oughta know. I was chief."

"Oh, yeah?"

"You need to get out of town, hear me? You're in too deep. I took care of that commando-nambo-pambo jerk, but there'll be more coming soon. Call your mom, you hear me? Go stay with her till things blow over."

"Kozmo, I wish you'd stop talking about my mom. I don't even know where she is, okay? She took off when I was a baby...probably back to England."

At the top of the hill, he halted. "Okay, so this is what I wanted to tell you, now that we're off their radar. I'll call my brother in the CIA. He'll check their database and find out where your mom is stationed. Then you'll go to her and be safe. She'll be briefed and waiting. I feel bad I can't come too. But if I left Madtown the whole world would collapse. It would be like Pandora's box, only worse." He spread out his arms, as if reaching to scoop up the expanse of Library Mall, State Street, the Capitol building. "One day all this will be mine. You know it, don't ya, baby?"

....

1995

When her dad got thrown in jail for his umpteenth DUI two years later, she withdrew all her savings and went straight to a travel agent. Before she knew it, she was arriving at Heathrow Airport in a leaden daze. Riding the tube into London, she viewed the clusters of weather-beaten row houses whizzing by and wondered if her mother had ridden this train when she'd ditched her husband and child to return to England twenty years ago. How had she felt? Sad? Or elated?

But now it was her stop. Earl's Court where, thanks to an old British drinking buddy of her dad's, she'd secured a job and lodging at the King's Head pub.

....

She'd only been at the pub a few weeks when she'd noticed an impish guy in a limp pinstripe suit watching her from a table as she sponged the bar top.

"Can I help you?" she said, approaching his table.

"I don't know, darling," he drawled in a husky sing-song, "Can you?"

"That's what I'm here for."

"Yes? I shall bear that in mind." He grinned at the dishrag in her hand. "Miss Cinderella."

She couldn't help but laugh. He was like some androgynous urchin from a musical, an aging Artful Dodger. "Slumming tonight?"

He frowned at his surroundings. "You know, I haven't the foggiest *how* I ended up here. Or...wait. I told my boss I was taking a long lunch. And it's been my lunch hour for…" He checked his watch. "…three days now."

"Seriously?"

As he chattered on, details emerged from the fog. Lunch had turned into an endless series of parties, bars and clubs. He hadn't slept in all that time, he claimed, lapping his glass of white wine. "Delaying the inevitable, aren't I? The inescapable monster come-down."

"One more day won't hurt," she smiled.

"Yes! Might as well treat myself to one last hurrah! It being a Friday, not to mention my birthday."

"Happy birthday," she said. "How old are you?"

"Gets to be rather a bore, doesn't it, keeping track of one's age." He pumped her hand. "Giles Justice." Then, nabbing a pen from her apron, he scribbled an address onto a cocktail napkin. "I'm having a little birthday do at my flat tonight. You absolutely *must* pop round."

....

"Miss Cinderella!" cried Giles, flinging open the door. As he helped her off with her—actually her dad's—old denim jacket, she took in all the chic, glittery people. Though a DJ spun dance tracks in the lounge, most people just stood around in stiff little cliques.

"So," he said, shoving her jacket into the arms of some pretty passing blonde, "was it frightfully long and boring, your cab ride up?"

"Oh, I took the tube."

"Did you *really*? How very *primitive*. You must be absolutely *gagging* for a drink."

She watched him flit off, then stepped from the path of a rowdy group pouring from a nearby door—a bathroom— sniffing and spilling drinks as they descended on the DJ, demanding tracks and shifting furniture. Then a strange sight caught her eye: a young woman in pigtails treading the carpet as if it were the moon, thanks to the springy devices strapped to her shoes.

"Hello, darling," purred the girl. "I'm Chloe. You a friend of Giles?"

"Sort of. I actually just met him today. Totally out of the blue."

"Sounds like our Giles." The girl peeled off her sweater. "One gets so bloody *hot* jumping about on these things, doesn't one? So what do you make of the do, darling?"

"It's really...decadent."

"Ah, decadence!" declared Giles, returning with a bottle of Moet and two glasses. "One of my two favorite 'd' words! The other being debauchery!"

Pushing away the offered glass, Chloe mimed powdering her nose. "You know I prefer my powders."

"She's *completely* deranged, our Chloe is," said Giles, shaking his head at her retreating half-clad form. "*Completely* off her tree. Enjoying yourself?"

She accepted her champagne with a nod. "The women are so pretty."

He turned to rummage through the drawers of a nearby table. No sooner had he produced a bag of white powder, a swarm of women materialized. "The noses on these girls!"

As the women pounced on the coke, she wandered into the kitchen where a statuesque black woman stood blowing smoke rings at the ceiling. "Alright?" greeted the woman.

"You look just like what's-her-face...that model, you know...Naomi Campbell."

The woman granted her a cool smile. "So I'm told."

Then an older, much shorter, sandy-bearded guy came into the kitchen. "Alright, darling?" he said to the Naomi clone.

"This is my boyfriend, Paolo," yawned the woman. "And I'm Imogen."

"Hi," she said.

The guy, in reply, waved a bag of powder in one hand, champagne bottle in the other.

Draining her champagne, she watched as the couple nosed coke from the countertop. When his girlfriend excused herself to the loo, the man, Paulo, finally acknowledged her. "American, I gather? Well, thank *Christ* you're not a Canadian. Americans might be obnoxious, but Canadians are abso-bloody-lutely *boring.* So what brought you to London, then?"

"My mom lives here." She lay a hand to her pulsing cheek. Hopefully she wouldn't have to explain how she hadn't even seen her mom; that though she'd tracked down an address, she kept putting off the big confrontation.

But the man wasn't interested. "Ever done any modeling?" he asked, sizing her up in one sidelong glance.

She flinched. Reek of gasoline and tires; smoke burning her throat; rhythmic clicking camera; screechy female laughter. SLUT. FREAK.

He handed her a business card. "My flat mate, as it happens, is a fashion photographer. He's doing a test shoot for models next Saturday. You should pop round."

"You mean, like, for free?"

"Mm," he nodded, refilling her champagne glass. "A bloody good photographer, him. It's how my Imogen got her start actually." He saluted Giles entering the kitchen. "Ah, the birthday boy."

Giles shook a baggie of white pills beneath her nose. "Party favor?"

"What is it?" she asked. "What does it do?"

"Just make you quite warm and fuzzy," said Giles, handing her a pill, "is all."

With a swill of champagne, she pretended to pop the pill, but slipped it into her jeans pocket instead.

Five minutes later, Giles found her in his bedroom, digging through a heap of jackets. "Alright, darling?"

"I gotta cruise," she said, gripping a gold-belted leopard-print coat. "It's getting late."

"Don't be daft. It's only just gone midnight." He eased the coat from her hands, marched her to the lounge and deposited her on a sofa. And, for the next hour or so, there she sat watching the revelers stomp about the room, whooping it up. Until in stormed Imogen, the supermodel lookalike: "Where the bloody hell's my jacket?"

She sagged back on the sofa, feigning sleep.

The boyfriend Paulo's voice then. "Never mind, darling. Someone probably took it home on accident. We'll sort it out tomorrow. Go home, shall we? I'm shattered."

"It had bloody well better turn up. Bloody Versace, that jacket. My favorite leopard print."

Then she must have actually dozed off, for when she opened her eyes, everyone had either vanished, or crashed on chairs and sofas.

After poking her head into several bedrooms, she found Giles alone on the back patio, puffing a cigar and watching the first flares of sunlight behind the panorama of sooty, embellished buildings, an archaic city alight. With a crooked smile, he held out the leopard-print coat. "Let's see about getting you home now, shall we? Before you turn into a pumpkin."

....

Mounting the doorstep of Paulo's flat the next Saturday, she took a moment to catch her breath before buzzing the bell. Kicking herself for popping that pill; which, instead of calming her nerves, had made her even shakier. Hand trembling, she jabbed the doorbell. What if he'd been messing with her about the photo shoot? What if he laughed in her face?

But, ushering her straight in, he indicated a spiral staircase. "Studio's down there."

Descending, she found herself in a blinding basement—lights everywhere, small ones strung along the ceiling, tall upstanding ones. But brightest of all: the blond man in the center of the room, dressed in a crisp white suit with his back to her. Fiddling with something. A camera.

Um," she said. "Hello?"

But he didn't turn around, just kept messing with his camera.

That hair, so blonde. The clothes, so white.

She clutched her throat. Reek of gasoline and tires; smoke burning her throat; rhythmically clicking camera.

....

1996

And now, one year later, here she is getting off the bus, headed for her mother's home in Camberwell. She knows where it is; she's walked by the dingy brick row house countless times. Even left a copy of the newspaper with her full-page Selfridges ad on the doormat once. Sometimes she stands across the street, leaning against a tree, watching for some sign of life from within—a switched-on light or twitch of a curtain.

But never anything. Always nothing.

Yet somehow she feels it in her bones: the presence inside. This time it will be different.

She walks up and rings the doorbell.

Here she stands on the doorstep, cheek flaring, head rushing from the pill, as she steels herself for the suddenly opened door, the woman's face: an older version on her own, maybe?

But: nothing.

Maybe the bell's broken. "Hello?" She's hammering the door now, so hard her knuckles throb. Stabbing the bell with her finger. "Hello?" Knocking. Buzzing. Banging. Shouting. Sobbing.

But the door doesn't open.

Party Town

Darrin Doyle

The party never stopped at Party Town. No matter the hour, day, or season, music blared from homes and apartments, where people danced and booze flowed. Classic rock, house beats, country, Latin jazz – whatever your taste, the only rule was to crank that shit. Solo cups littered lawns, sprinkled like red candies amid cornhole boards, sofas, and beer pong tables. Folks wandered the streets, house to house, searching for more and finding it. Old, young, black, white, fat, thin – they were all invited and they all came. Little kids zipped around, playing tag as their parents got wasted. For as long as anyone could remember it had been this way. They were exhausted, sure, but having a ton of fun. Sleep was allowed if you needed it, which everyone eventually did, but they all got used to nodding off to the thump of bass and the squeals of happy revelers.

They'd heard about other towns where people had jobs and went to school and volunteered for soup kitchens. The residents of Party Town thought, *Nasty!* Those things didn't sound fun. *Have a good time!* was their motto. Life was too short to be monkeying around with shit like that. Sure, sometimes people in Party Town got sick or died, but that was no reason not to keep partying. If you couldn't make lemonade out of lemons, you might as well be a tadpole or something. They were put here on Earth to live, dammit, and they were going to live. Funerals were even bigger parties than everyday parties because they wanted to show God or whoever was up there that *Hey, you aren't going to stop our fun, asshead!*

Nobody was sure, or could remember, where their food came from, or why they had power in their homes and gasoline in their cars, or whom to thank for the endless supply of wine, beer, and spirits. Whenever the topic came up, they would shrug and say, *Who the hell cares?* The less they thought about stuff like this, the better.

As the decades passed, the partying took a toll. Children, teens, and adults – they were all pretty haggard. Most were addicted to alcohol and cigarettes, and in some cases, narcotics. Men's bellies bloated; women's, too. Bad skin all around. Flabby, weak, and foggy-minded people. Lots of STDs: you name it, they had it. Fistfights, dramatic screaming matches. Lack of sleep and poor diet meant long-term issues like hepatitis and bone degeneration. Life expectancy kept shrinking, babies born with fetal alcohol syndrome, whatever. The people didn't get sad about this stuff. It was just the way it was. Whenever a person pointed out the problems in Party Town, another would be there to say, *There's always been problems, throughout history! We just like to* think *we have it worse now. It's so egotistical.*

Then they would hug tearfully and say, *Wow, remember how we always heard that life is short? Well it really is, man. It really is.* And they would raise their glasses and toast. And they would party even harder, in daylight and darkness.

We Don't Have to Decide Anything Now

Drew Buxton

I FELT LIKE:
Every time I see you it's for the first time.

Grateful for our time.

But I hate you,
and I feel like:
Taking a shit in the toilet
and leaving it for you to find
and getting defensive
before you can get mad.

I want you to hate me
the way I hate you sometimes.

I want you to hate me
and spend your time thinking about me,

deciding what's good and what's bad.

I want you to want to fuck me up,
I want you to fuck me up.

What if one day you just showed up
uninvited
and fucked me?
I would be so happy.

But I think I turned on you,
sometime
after we had fun.

A Good Tombstone

Joseph G. Peterson

"Let me tell you a story," I say. Tina and I are on the road and she hasn't given me directions yet. She hasn't told me where she wants to go but she wants to go somewhere. I'm driving her car down the main road leading out of town and I'm really not in any shape to drive. Tina isn't speaking. She's as silent as a clam. To break the silence I tell her the first thing that pops into my mind. "Let me tell you a story," I say, "to cheer you up. Let me tell you, Tina, about this man I used to know."

Tina looks at me, then looks out the window at the passing road.

"I used to know this guy," I say. "His name was Stoshy. Actually it was Herman Stosh, but everybody called him Stoshy, even the old timers. Even the young timers. He was an old retired man with traces of yellow hair still growing on his head. Actually I think he was part Norwegian or Swedish or something—I do know, however, that he was born here in the States near the beginning of the century. He was a squarely built man, an old farmer sort. He had these strong hands with stout fingers. You should have seen them. I mean if hands could tell stories—right—oh yes and his eyes too—they were really something else. I mean I used to wonder whether he had cataracts or something because his eyes, which were primarily blue, also seemed flat—it was almost as if he were blind or something, though certainly wasn't blind. I mean he could see well enough to do his job—to bag groceries. Anyway it was funny because the flatness in his eyes was usually offset by a protruding unlit cigar that he almost always had clenched between his teeth. I don't know if he ever smoked his cigars or just chewed on them. Once in a while I'd see him in the parking lot pushing grocery carts, but even then, he'd keep his cigar unlit. Anyway, before he became a bag clerk at the grocery store he used to do something else—some sort of factory job or something. Something having to do with metal—with aluminum or something. I know that. But before the factory job he was a truck farmer right here in town. He used to grow squash and sweet corn—that kind of thing—and sell it at the markets downtown. But that was before most of the homes that are here now, were here. I mean that was probably in the Forties or something. But after farming—I mean the farming ended up being a real failure; I think he sold his land to a bank for a loss— he took this job in the factory and he worked there for years and then he retired and for a while he was enjoying his retirement, and then tragedy struck: his wife died. They'd been married maybe fifty years or so. Anyway after she died he took this job as a bagger at the grocery store in order to fill up the empty time, and also to keep sociable, to keep in touch with people. Of course, I learned of all this over time, because you see, Stoshy he was sort of a proud man. I mean you'd think he was a proud man on account of the fact that he was both polite and reserved and on account of the fact that he did his job so professionally—but in actuality I mean once you got to know him—he was really quite approachable—a very likable man and it wasn't long before we became friends. The one thing I remember about Stoshy was that he liked to play the lottery. It was a sort of obsession with him. So every time I was at the grocery store, while my stuff was being rung up at the cash register he and I would talk. 'Hey Stoshy,' I'd ask him. 'Do you have good numbers this week?' Every week he'd give me the same answer. He would say in a soft but gruff sort of voice: 'No, no. I got the same numbers I had last week.' He would then add: 'You know Abe, a ticket ain't no good unless it wins. Until then, all numbers are bad.' Nevertheless, he would continue to play the same numbers every week. Every week, he used the phone number of the laundromat across from the grocery store. The number was painted in gold letters on the laundromat window and he looked at it every day he was in the parking lot collecting grocery carts. Anyway, one week the lottery was worth twenty-five million or something like that. I mean it was the largest lottery in state history. I don't think it's ever been that high before or since. I mean, lottery fever just swept across the state. I even bought a lottery ticket, and I'm not even a gambler. Well I knew Stoshy must have been primed about the unprecedented jackpot. So I asked him, as usual, if he had picked any good numbers that week. He looked at me and said: 'I have a feeling I'm going to win, Abe. For this jackpot I decided to try something different. That old number has never done me any good, and I want to win this time.' So I asked him. I said: 'What are you gonna do if you win?' 'If I win,' he said, 'I'm gonna buy a large double tombstone for my wife and I. You know, the one she has now, is not so good. She was a good lady and she deserves a good tombstone. I want to get one for us together, the best money can buy. And I want to put an inscription on it. And I want the inscription to say: I never gave up on you in life. I never gave up on you in death. She knows I never gave up on her. But other people should know too.' Then I joked with him and said: 'You don't need twenty-five million for that. You just need a few hundred.' But he turned to me and said in all seriousness: 'Abe, I need twenty-five million just to get started doing the things I want to do.' Anyway, the next week, after the lottery drawing, I went to the grocery store to see how Stoshy did. When he saw me walk into the store, he burst out crying. 'What happened, Stoshy, why are you crying? Did you lose the lottery?' He shook his head yes, but couldn't speak because he was all choked up. 'Stoshy, what's wrong,' I said. I put my hand on his shoulder. 'I lost,' he said. 'I did something different this time. I played her birthdate and mine, just like. . .' And he didn't say it, but it occurred to me, his birthdate and hers, just like you'd have on a tombstone. 'And the number that won this time. . .' Stoshy pointed to the phone number that was painted on the window of the laundromat across the street. 'My old number. Ten years I have that number. Ten years, every week I have that number and I look at it every day and now when I change it, it wins. I cannot believe it.' He lifted his arms and said: 'I can't talk about it anymore.' Of course Stoshy was never the same after that. He died two months later of a stroke. Actually the store manager had stopped me just after he died and asked if I would mind terribly, but they needed one more pallbearer at Stoshy's funeral. We buried him right next to his wife, and like her he had a very ordinary tombstone. It just said: 'Herman Stosh 1908-1995'."

"Wow," Tina says. "Is that true?"

"Pretty much. Yes, I say. It's pretty much true."

"That's terrible Abe," she says at last. "What do you think?"

"What do you mean, what do I think?"

"Do you think he and his wife are together now?"

"I don't know," I say. "It's possible. Anything's possible."

"Abe, don't stop driving," Tina says. "Please, just keep going and let's stop when we stop. How about that—is that ok? I don't feel like stopping tonight."

"That's ok," I say.

"I don't want to go home right now. I just want to be able to close my eyes and pretend like I'm going somewhere—somewhere far away from here. Can we do that Abe?"

"Yes," I say. "Yes, we can do that."

Perfume

Rachel Slotnick

I OPENED A jar of my grandmother's
perfume
17 years after her funeral,
and there she stood, disapproving,
5'1" and wide-hipped,
inhaling the plumes of her Charleston
cigarette in my living room,
ashing on my succulents.

Pancakes smell of my first love, resting his
bare feet on the dining room table.
His powdered sugar thumbprints, perfectly
preserved fossils of his prehistoric
manners, dapple the chairs, the furniture,
my hips.

Oil and metal evoke my father tinkering in
the garage,

constructing towers from flashlights. Try
as I might to forget the cacophony,
I can still hear him madly hammering, and
machines whirring under the silent moon.

& then there's me
& I don't know what I smell like.
They say you can't ever smell yourself,
really.
You need someone else's nose
To become a bottle of memory.

The Honeymoon Suite

Alice Kaltman

Jitters

I watch my daughter examine herself in the Honeymoon Suite mirror. She looks idiotic—not that I would ever let her know—with that fake lilac headband and fluffy veil, her bosom spilling out of her gown like two mounds of vanilla ice cream. Adele's a big gal. Takes after my Swedish Nebraskan family, though I myself have always been a string bean. Luckily her curves are proportional. Plus she inherited Kurt's good looks, his wavy blonde hair, straight nose, and killer smile. Adele was spared my horsey plainness, though I'd like to think she inherited a bit of my good sense.

"This is a mistake," Adele moans, then pouts. The red lipstick gives her a demented kewpie doll look. I'm not sure what mistake she's referring to: the veil, the dress, or the whole wedding. I keep quiet.

Adele puts her hands on her waist and squeezes. I can see the strain in her arm muscles. She can barely breathe.

"Stop that Sweetie," I say. "You look beautiful."

I walk unsteadily in my high heels to the king-sized bed and sit to take a load off. It's a bed for giants. Rich football stars. All I've ever had is a queen. Plenty big for me solo, now that Kurt drinks himself to sleep in the den most nights, TV blaring. I find him spread-eagle and disheveled on the couch come morning.

Kurt and I went to Puerto Vallarta for our honeymoon. He was up for anything. I loved that about him back then. I happily deferred while he struck up conversations with strangers. We spent an entire day with one couple named Carlos and Lupe. Lupe had a pet parrot she found more interesting than humans, especially me. She'd kiss that noisy squawker, lips to beak, which seemed highly unsanitary to me. They spoke Spanish to each other, none of which I understood. The words sounded obscene, especially the bird's.

There was lots of tequila that day, something I wasn't used to. I'd worn my favorite red vest with the black trim, but took it off because of the drinking and the heat. I forgot it in the back of a taxi, a clackety-clack clown car that would never pass inspection here in the States.

Carlos passed out after lunch. Kurt and Lupe danced off together after supper. Kurt came back to our hotel room after midnight, sheepish and apologetic. Lying the first of many lies. Or the first one I caught.

"Josh is good for you," I say to Adele as I lie back on the bed and stare up at the mirrored ceiling. Honeymoon Suite, here they come. "He's dependable."

"As. In. Boring." She's squeezing her waist again.

"That's not what I mean," I say. But maybe it is what I mean. Kurt was far from boring and look where that got me. I wonder how things go for Adele and Josh in the sack. But this is not the kind of subject I ever discuss with my daughter. Or with anyone, really. "Let's just say Josh is not going to throw you under any buses."

Adele turns her head from side to side. "Do you think the diamond earrings are overkill?"

"Keep them. They're fantastic," I lie. After many years I've picked up a few tricks.

Joy

Helen's sweaty from her jog along the lake, needs a shower desperately, but that can wait. Meanwhile, the door is reluctant, unobliging. If she knocks, John, wheezing and gray-faced, will trudge across the thickly carpeted floor to let her in. And that won't do. Instead, she dips the swipe card in this way, that way, this again, waiting for the green light. "Fucking excuse for a key," Helen mutters, sure that the maid who's passing by with towel-loaded cart thinks Helen's a lunatic, or worse, an entitled bitch. Finally, the card bids her entry and Helen pushes the ponderous door open.

John sits in the easy chair, the murder mystery Helen bought him a few weeks prior splayed open on his lap. It makes sense that her husband would choose that god-awful chair. He's spent too many days prone, wasting away in the all-the-bells-and-whistles hospital bed they'd installed in the spare bedroom back home. Helen eyes the cushy, satin-covered king-sized bed in this Honeymoon Suite, and nearly salivates with desire. Oh, to lie down and drift off in a catatonic stupor, she thinks. But no. This weekend is about engagement, so Helen must remain alert.

John hasn't read any of the book. It has been splayed at exactly the same mid-spine spot for days. We're both pretending, she thinks and joins his charade. "Johnny, you'll never guess what I saw on my run," she giggles, believably. "It was hysterical. Totally Chaplin-esque."

She plops on the bed to gaze up at the mirrored ceiling. It's easier to maintain peppiness staring at her own reflection than to look at what remains of her husband.

John exiles the unread book to the side table. "Tell me," he says, his crackled voice a rasp against her heart.

Helen remains light. "There was this woman walking a golden retriever. The dog's pulling her along, and she can barely stay upright, what with a gazillion paper shopping bags knocking against her body."

"Ouch," says John.

"Exactly," Helen agrees. "Then another woman and little girl come ambling up from the opposite direction. The girl is probably around five or six. Definitely a mother and daughter. You know, coloring, body language."

"Like you and Sasha when she was little," John remembers, "Your own mini-me."

Helen studies her reflection, a crumpled, faded version of their daughter, now twenty-eight years old, living in Los Angeles, single, defensive, but gainfully employed. Helen used to worry about her bristly daughter all the time, but John takes up all the anxiety parking spots now.

"Even more mini-me-ish than Sash and me," Helen says. "They were in matching outfits.

Awful chartreuse fleece hoodies and striped leggings. Ugg boots."

"Ugh is right," John whispers.

He's punning, thinks Helen. That's good. We're on a roll.

Then John coughs. A wet, gurgly sound. An incessant, internal seepage that usually undoes Helen. But today, she's determined to keep her cool.

"Hold on, hold on," Helen dashes to grab him tissues. The bathroom is enormous. Obscene. There are two sinks, a heart-shaped Jacuzzi tub, lotions and potions for all body parts in a red rattan basket near the bidet. Helen resists the urge to fill the tub, strip off her rancid workout gear and plunge in, jets pummeling her flesh at full blast. Later maybe, she hopes. There are ribbed condoms with hotel insignia embossed on rose-colored foil, nestled like candies in their own special basket next to the tissue box. By booking the Honeymoon Suite, she'd wanted to give the weekend a romantic patina. But if John happened upon these? Overkill, she thinks. Cruel. She shoves the condom basket under the sink, behind a strawberry scented candle that assaults her with saccharine fumes as she shuts the cabinet door.

John is lying on the bed when she returns. He's staring at his reflection, his face a grimacing ashen mask. He's a bag of loose, wobbly objects jumbled inside sweatpants and sweatshirt. Shriveled here, bloated there. Helen places the tissue box gingerly in the concave dip that used to be John's flabby stomach. Who needs a TV tray? John joked, just last week, as he snacked on pretzels from the same spot.

Helen lies down beside him. "Where was I?" She grabs his ice-cold hand.

"How the hell would I know?" John's testy. He blames the medication, but really, he hasn't had patience for her stories in years. "Something about a kid and her mother in ugly clothes. Before that, something about a big dog and grocery bags."

Why do I even try? Helen wants to say. Even when dying, you're a nasty son of a bitch. But she's a bulldozer and continues with extra verve. "So, the mom is also loaded with grocery bags, and her kid has an ice cream cone. The kid sees the dog and jumps for joy. She starts running towards the dog and the dog starts tugging on its leash to get to her."

"Sounds like a shit show," says John, "When does it get funny?"

Helen squeezes his hand hard. She wants to crush it, feel his bones splinter. She has impulses like this quite often, ones she would never, or at least hasn't, acted upon. She imagines shards turning to chalk within the sack of his skin. Along with these impulses, Helen also has Let's get on with this death thing already thoughts. But more often, she has When you go, the hole in my life will be so enormous I just might have to jump in it and disappear myself thoughts. I love you thoughts.

Helen sighs. "Come on. Let me finish."

John closes his eyes and nods, feebly.

"The dog owner loses her grip on the leash and the dog skitters towards the kid," Helen's so chipper, it's like she's channeled an entire cheerleading squad. "Both women run behind their separate charges with bags swinging away. Then the bags start ripping. Produce goes flying, granola hits the pavement, eggs go splat, tomatoes explode, milk streams everywhere." She pauses for effect.

"That's it?" John coughs again.

You usually love slapstick, Helen thinks, releasing her husband's hand. This tidbit has all the right elements of mayhem and buffoonery, of near disaster belonging to someone else. "No, there's more. The dog reaches the little girl and nips the ice cream cone out of her hand and devours the entire thing," Helen's talking so fast she sounds like a speed freak. "The silly beast's snout is covered in chocolate. By the time the women get there, the dog is slobbering chocolate kisses all over the kid's face, the two of them as happy as can be. The End."

John wheezes, but says nothing.

You're supposed to be laughing, you old grump, Helen thinks. "Most kids would've been reduced to tears." She can see his deflated chest rise and fall next to her out of the corner of her eye. "Sash would've been whiny for the rest of the day at that age."

"It's bad for dogs," John opens his eyes and takes a tissue to wipe phlegmy residue from the corners of his cracked lips.

"What the fuck, Johnny," Helen pounds the satin bedspread in frustration. "How can a child's love be bad for a dog?"

John lies still as stone, maybe practicing for the inevitable. "Not love. Chocolate. It's toxic. If dogs eat too much of it they can die."

The air is molten, but John can't tolerate air conditioning anymore, and the Honeymoon Suite windows don't open. The mirrored ceiling doppelgangers stare down at Helen and John and they stare back. Everyone gasps for breath.

Her Giant Sequoia

If only Ryan could stop crying, but the damn tears keep coming, gushing like geysers, dribbling down hot cheeks, rivulets in the creases of his quivering jowls. Ryan hasn't bawled like this since he was a kid. He's heaving relentless sobs that feel lethal, like an asthmatic gasping for breath. But Ryan's not ill; he's just pathetic. He's already soaked the pocket square he'd folded—just in case—in the inner pocket of his tuxedo. Now he clutches that damp and useless rag in a trembling hand. He's too stunned to get off his ass and grab tissues from the obscenely huge, strawberrystenched bathroom of the Honeymoon Suite. Ryan had been prepared to cry on this momentous day, his wedding day, four days shy of his twenty-fifth birthday, the day he and Julie were to bind themselves like twisted ribbons. Knotted at both ends. Together forever. But Ryan had anticipated tears of joy, of ecstatic release, not these clucking wails. He sounds like one of his grandpa's chickens, careening around the barnyard trying to avoid the old bastard's hatchet.

There's no end in sight for these sputtering sobs. They keep pounding him, like an opposing team's defensive line. Ryan sinks to the floor, his cummerbund a vise grip as he doubles over sturdy haunches.

"Tree trunks," Julie had sighed stroking his linebacker thighs a mere two nights before, "My very own Giant Sequoia."

What did Ryan expect, falling in love with a girl raised by hippies on a commune outside Bolinas? Home-schooled, but not really schooled at all, she talked about chakras and carried a dog-eared copy of The Essential Rumi wherever she went. Ryan almost understood the poems, which Julie liked to read aloud after sex, but not really. Nothing Julie ever said made much sense. What made sense was how she held Ryan captive with those sighs, that magic tongue, her model looks. Her boobs for god's sake, what a pair. What made sense to Ryan was Julie choosing him over those other dudes. She'd confessed about them all. Man-bunned Hank the barista, with a

Popeye tattoo on his minuscule bicep and a ring through his schnoz. Banker Chet, who scurried around San Fran on a dorky recumbent bike. Elliot, the egghead from Harvard who did some-kind-of-something that was pure gobbledygook to Ryan. When Julie explained it, Ryan nodded and aha'd, pretending.

The competition was laughable, or so Ryan assumed. After all, he was her Giant Sequoia. Julie's hunky football-playing big lug with a pro-ball contract. A millionaire by way of grunting, passing, sweating, running, colliding, and assaulting. Her massive man who offered rescuing hands to tackled compadres and opponents alike. Genuinely nice, the kind of guy who glugged Gatorade from a spigot attached to a plastic tub, but always made sure to leave enough swigs for the next thirsty beast.

 For over an hour, the wedding guests had to sit in the pews, fidgeting as they watched Ryan stare down the aisle, wiping droplet after droplet of sweat from his shelf-like brow. All of them waiting for Julie to be escorted by Willow and Raven, her dimwit stoner parents with no brain cells left after all the pot they'd grown, smoked, sold. Then Ryan looked up at the guests from his buzzing phone and said in a flailing, choked voice careening across two octaves,

"The wedding is off, folks. You can all go on home."

They scurried out of the church like a bunch of released convicts.

In the end, Egghead Elliot scored the touchdown. Now Ryan sits in this Honeymoon Suite alone, leaning massive shoulders against the satin spread of a bed made for the likes of him. A king-sized atrocity, a squishy, bouncy crash pad for fucking, for fermenting in newlywed juices. Instead, this jilted giant is deeper in his own cavernous stew.

Maid Service

Snooping through opened luggage, lingerie on the floor, or the goopy residue on room service trays tells me only so much. I know the whole story after the lovers have gone for good, when all that's left are their scents, invisible fumes, whiffs of the essential. More often than not, the air in here is ripe with desire. But sometimes the place is filled with a mournful stench. I've gotten more than one nose full of despair.

The minute I pushed my cart through the door just now, I could tell that last couple had quite a racy time. Her scent mixed with his. Like my abuela's backyard: cilantro and wet mutt. Kind of nasty, right? But it's a loving stink.

Which smell is hers and which is his? Your guess is as good as mine. Fumes all over the place from those two, even behind that ugly upright chair. Their smells are never separate, which tells me what I need to know.

They don't know how lucky they are. Or maybe they do.

When Carlos was an infant, I had to bring him to work a bunch of times. It was right after Freddy left me. Left us. I figured out a way to hide Carlos from that bitch supervisor, Roberta. I wedged his little body between stacks of towels, rolled my cart down the halls like I was pushing a pyramid of crystal goblets, each nubby carpet bump a possible disaster. Carlos slept most of the time back then, which was lucky. Thank God he stayed quiet. When I got in each room, I'd take him out and lay him in the center of the bed. This king-sized was the best, even if he woke up. I'd plop him in the center and watch him wiggle his little brown arms and legs, like an upside down beetle. So happy. Laughing like a crazy drunken fool staring up at his reflection in that porno ceiling. This bed is so huge I didn't have to worry about him sliding off the edge. I could clean the whole place without that freaked out lump in my throat, my heart beating like a tom-tom drum, which was how it was in all the regular rooms.

Maybe that's why I'm so good at reading the vibe in here. Maybe I'm psychic. I have good associations with this humongous Honeymoon Suite, with its big-ass bed, giant vat of a bathtub, and embarrassing mirrored ceiling.

So, you want to know more about that last couple? I give them two years tops. A baby will come. They'll each love that baby with such smelly sweetness. They'll make two new perfumes, each a blend with that baby. But this odor? This soppy dog and cilantro scent? This sexy funk? Breathe deep, my friend. This may be the last of it, right here.

The House in the Pines

Steve Karas

The constant buzzing of cicadas like high-voltage power lines is one of the things I'll remember most about this little house in the pine forest. Maybe because day and night it reminds me I'm not alone, keeps me from getting lost in my thoughts. *Why here?* I can't stop asking myself. *How did he end up here, across the ocean, up and over endless mountain ranges, in this secret corner of the world? And what did I expect to find?*

I head down to the small beach at the foot of the hill where a man with leathery skin serves fresh fish out of a shack. When I sit down at a table, the legs of the wooden chair sink into the pebbles. I pick at brined anchovies, slices of cucumber and tomato. I sip on a glass of homemade wine, feel it burn its way down my throat.

A gray dog, the whites of his eyes stained yellow, rests beside me in the shade. I can make out each of his ribs. "Here boy," I say, and toss him a fried smelt. He gobbles it up, then looks at me, waits, before resting his head back down and staring off into the distance.

An old couple sneaks up from behind the pine trees, carrying beach chairs, carefully stepping on the pebbles so they don't slip. We're the only ones here, the five of us including the dog. *Why did he choose this place over us? This place he'd never been to before, this place where he had no ties?* I light a cigarette and ash into a big seashell. Maybe the old couple knew my father. They probably did, but I can't bring myself to ask.

....

The house in the pine forest is not mine, or wasn't originally, at least. It was my father's. He disappeared here after my mother passed. We don't know how he found it or why. They enjoyed taking their trips, but they'd never been to this part of the world together, certainly not here. They never told us that was the plan. That if one of them died, the other would disappear in a far-off corner of the Earth. That if we lost one of them, we'd lose the other one as well.

The house is at the top of a hill you get to only by following a winding road overgrown with shrubs. There are no neighbors in sight, but sometimes I hear reggae music or the kick-starting of a moped. Through the trees, there is a view of the sea spreading forth like a road to God knows where.

The cicadas buzz into the night. I have trouble falling sleep. Dogs bark madly for hours like two packs of wolves fighting to the death. I wonder if the gray dog with yellow eyes is among them. I hope he is not. I think about what I'm going to do with this little house in the pines, the closest thing I have to my father's beating heart. When I almost drift off, a mosquito cries into my ear, fills its body with my blood.

....

I drive down the winding road, through the countryside and into town. Weeds jet from cracks in the pavement. Stray dogs rifle through trash bins. I have the name and address of a lawyer who is supposed to speak English, who I hope will help me figure out what to do. When I get to town, though, everything is closed. The cafés, the market, even the travel agency at the port where ferry boat tickets are sold. The lawyer is not in. I don't know what day it is or if it's a holiday. I panic, maybe from jet lag or sleep deprivation, imagine I've stumbled into some parallel universe. I'm going to disappear here just like my father.

I drive back to the small beach thinking I'll ask the man with the leathery skin if he knows what's going on today, but the shack is closed too. I spot the gray dog resting in the shade of a bamboo thatch umbrella, and it gives me peace. He ambles over when he sees me and lays at my feet, face against his paws. The sand conforms to his bony body. I decide to name him Pilgrim because he reminds me of my father. My father who was on a journey to this place of apparent significance, though I still haven't figured out what that is.

I pick up a green piece of glass smoothed by the ocean's waves and skip it across the water's surface. I take a swim. The sea is thick and calm like olive oil. *After Mom died, did he not want us to see him deteriorate?* Pilgrim's eyes close, so I whistle for his attention, make sure he doesn't leave me here.

....

Back at the house in the pines, I take a cold shower, taste the salt sliding from my hair and face and over my lips. My shorts dry in the sun. I get out and walk around the house. The dust and dirt on the floor are gritty against my feet. There is always dust and dirt on the floor no matter how many times I sweep.

I come across a travel book hidden in one of the bedroom drawers. The book is about this part of the world. This secret corner. My mother has written on the inside of the cover. *This book is a promise that we will one day travel to this beautiful land I have dreamt so much about. A promise that it will be our last stop, where we can dissolve into the sea or sky when it is our time to depart the Earth.* I sit at the edge of the bed and read it over and over. My father's telescope is pointed out the window at the clouds. A star chart is taped to the wall. It makes me think how far we sometimes are from those we are closest to.

At night I sit on the balcony and drink wine I found in a cupboard. The cicadas continue to call. Somewhere in the dark I can hear the packs of dogs fighting to survive. Pilgrim wanders up to the house. I don't know how he found me in this pine forest. Maybe he followed the jaundiced half-moon hanging above, so big it looks like you can touch it. I go inside and cut from a loaf of bread on the counter. I throw it to Pilgrim and he licks it up, then puts his head back down. My father has left an open stepladder on the balcony. I finish my glass of wine and climb to the top rung, reach for the moon, see if there's something, anything, I can grab on to.

Deon Dreyer, Bushman's Hole

Gerald Brennan

I'VE BEEN WAITING for you here

These ten dark and lonely years

Half as long now as I lived

Mom and dad had to give up hope

Of seeing me again

They dried their tears up long ago

I know

You know

They still think about me, though

There's a plaque that bears my name

Somewhere up there in the air

No way to see it here

In my underwater night

My light was on when I went down

My friends saw it fading, deep

It felt like I fell asleep

I blacked out before I drowned

The bulb stayed on a day or so

A glow in this crystal void

Is it a cathedral or a tomb?

So much space

The longest peace

Until your light cut through the gloom

Did you know

You'd find me here

In these waters dark and clear?

If you were surprised, it didn't show

An uninvited guest

You do your best

To take me with you

Dare to lift me

Unprepared

It's too hard though

You know you can't stay long

Your actions give excuses

Once you see I don't come loose

You check your watch

It's time to go

You leave me lying on my back

Before too long I'm back in black

But you've tied a string to me

So we both know

That you'll be back

You tell everyone you've met about me

Some sights you can't forget

You're not up there long, I see

Just time to tot up what you've learned

And plot your next return

How you'll bag me, take me there

To the world of open air

I remember what it looked like:

Sunlight on the grassy plains

Zebras, lions, antelopes

And their last mortal remains

That's all that remains of me

Just a carcass out of place

In the darkness

And a rubber suit and mask

You ask my parents

If they'd like to bury me

It's very easy for you

To understand their pain

A Christian man

You've got a wife

Two kids of your own

A life

Something I never wanted

Or I wanted too much to keep

We both loved the same adventures

And the lure of the haunted deep

I don't deserve the effort

You want to save me but there's nothing
left to save

And nothing for you to do but move me
from grave to grave

Still you come back, why?

You think you know

All you need to know to go

Down here and work, fine

Only for a minute, though

I see a line

And then your light

Fall into my endless night

You see me again

My only friend

It seems

In your dreams

You dreamed of this

But now your mind

Feels full of wine

A dark and harmful bliss

Something's amiss

Pressure cracks most things down here

These are just the simple facts

Where a man cannot relax

How can a man survive?

Surprise

My heart is made of wax

I am lighter than you think

Your camera films your final acts

Fingers fumble

Like you've had another drink

You think foggy now

You stumble

Slip on slime

Check your watch

Hey, look at the time!

What a crime

But it seems

Most things get tangled in the dark

Our hopes, our dreams

Our ropes

Your hope's alive

But you can't cut

You breathe hard

You're on your guard

Is that fear now in your gut?

You fall asleep against your will

Your light's still bright but now it's still

And now another's high above

You've met your end

Is this a friend

You dearly love

Coming down now to share it?

His love pushing down his fear

Three's a crowd, it might get loud

But do we hear a click, a crack?

Too much pressure for his gear

He must know he must go back

And so we stay

And in a day

Your light, too, it fades to black

Then there's a tug

From an unseen hand

Who understands?

How we float up towards the land of land

At first we spend

A night in a cave

While your wife dreams of an empty grave

Your friends speak of being brave

And then sing Amazing Grace

Near this rocky water place

We feel something

After they sing

Are they able now to bring

Us up this final bit?

This goal you sought with all your might

Now happening

By their hands?

That's sometimes how it goes

We make demands

And plans

To set things right

And it all comes to naught

But when we don't do a thing

Somehow it happens without a fight

Someone cuts these knotted strings

And we fall up into the light

Three Men on a Boat

Darrin Doyle

They began with hope. Piles of fish, they imagined, would fill the deck. Salmon, trout, sturgeon, pike, whatever they could get their hooks in. They weren't picky because they just loved being out on the open lake, together. Best buddies for many years, domestic obligations in the form of wives, children, and careers had made it practically fricking impossible to get together.

When are we going to do some fishing! they liked to write in emails, when they had the chance to email.

None of them could answer this question. Years passed. Their main way of staying in touch was checking out social media photos and observing the growth and accomplishments of each others' children: new teeth; cool rockets built and launched; awkward dance get-ups and big braces; regional volleyball tournaments; sunburns and crutches. They were proud of one another and couldn't believe how damn old they were all getting!

Once the children were out of high school and the wives had settled back into their careers and the men were in positions of authority at their jobs, granting them flexibility in choosing vacation dates, they finally found the time to go out and *get this thing done.*

The men all had quit smoking and cut back on (not quit!) drinking, but for this weekend they bought cigarettes and hard liquor and beer and agreed that this was going to be fucking fun. Christ, they'd earned it.

One of the men, whose name was Bill, owned the 30-foot fishing boat. Bill didn't like calling it a boat, however: he called it a *vessel*.

"This vessel's been good to me," he said when they boarded. "She's temperamental, though."

"Like all the women in your life, Billy," Carl joked.

"But what's up with the name?" Jack said.

The vessel was named *Huge Pen Is*.

"Don't like it?" Billy asked.

"I guess it's fine," Jack agreed.

Billy gave them a full tour: "10-inch Navnet, black box sounder, 600-watt transducer, hardtop outriggers, front and side curtains all up in here, fridge, stove, microwave, leg-mounted rod holders, sweet little cow pulpit, power steering, live well, toilet, sink, shower, stereo with satellite."

"You done good, Billy," the other men agreed.

After lunch at the dock they motored far out onto Lake Michigan. The sky was drawn with a stringy white cloud like a milk mustache on the face of God. Gentle waves swatted at the *Huge Pen Is* as it carved a gentle path across the sparkling blue expanse. The wake trailed like a foamy serpent that would try and try but never quite overtake them.

"WOO!" Billy yelled, his hair windswept.

"WOO!" the other men answered.

They toasted with Styrofoam cups of Jack Daniels. The sun blazed high, naked and joyous. Forty miles out they dropped anchor and set their lines.

"Hope the cocksucking fish are biting," Jack said. At home he was careful not to use profanities. His wife didn't mind, but their wildly religious housekeeper found such language disturbing.

"Who cares either way," Carl said. "I'm just jacked to be out here with you guys. You're my dudes."

"Buds forever," Billy said.

"Buds," said Jack.

They drank another toast and a few more.

Hours passed with no bites. The boat rocked like a lazy cradle.

"This is so sweet," Carl said.

Many years – decades, really – had spread between the men, and yet such a comfort and familiarity remained that they felt no need to ask questions about careers, wives, children, television shows. They fell asleep in their seats under the warm sun.

Billy woke first. "Dang it, we missed the sunset," he said.

"Missed the sunset!" Jack screamed. He'd jolted awake and knocked his glass onto the deck, spilling a few gulps of Jack.

"We should prank Carl like we used to," Billy giggled.

They looked at Carl, who was snoring with his lips parted.

"Put something weird in his mouth," Jack suggested.

"I got a better idea. Let's flip him into the water."

"He can swim, can't he?"

"Used to be on the swim team if I remember correctly."

"Remember when they all shaved their heads and thought it was cool."

"Wasn't it cool?"

"I guess. Didn't impress me much."

"Got the girls all hot."

"Pff, girls."

"You grab that leg and I'll grab this one, and then whoopsy doo, he'll go flying out into the water."

"Hee hee."

"I can't believe we're doing this!"

"Hurry, he's waking up."

On the count of three Jack and Billy heaved. "He's too fat!"

They couldn't do much other than raise Carl a few inches off his seat. He woke up looking confused and irritated. Billy grabbed at his back. "Jeez, I popped something. Dammit, that hurt." He paced the deck, wincing and twisting.

"You guys trying to dump me?" Carl said groggily.

"If you weren't such a lardo you'd be in the water right now," Jack laughed.

"Good thing you didn't. I don't know how to swim."

"You weren't on the swim team?"

"No."

"We thought you were."

Billy started shouting and pointing as he hobbled toward the bow. "Bite! Bite!"

The tip of one of the rods was wiggling. Jack clambered to it, arriving ahead of Billy, and pulled the rod from its holder. He reeled and heaved, shoulders straining, leaning back and forward in a rhythmic action, the rod bent fiercely like a clawed finger.

"Bring that sucker in!" Carl clapped and hooted.

"Don't lose it, Jack."

Jack was huffing, cheeks tremoring with every breath. Sweat poured down his face. "Wipe me!" he cried, and Billy toweled his face like a welterweight trainer so his pal wouldn't have to stop the fight. Carl started snapping photos with his cell phone, but they were coming out pretty dark so he put his phone away.

The fish would not surrender. Jack refused to take a break. He needed to land this beast. He imagined the enormous mounted fish hanging triumphantly over his fireplace for many years. He imagined his two sons at his funeral, getting into wrestling match as they argued over who would take possession of the beautiful salmon or whatever. He decided he would bequeath his trophy to the local library along with a donation so they would name a section of shelves after him.

"Holy crap your face is red," Billy said. He was now seated, tired from watching and waiting, drowsy from the booze, a little angry that this was taking so long. What the heck time was it, anyway?

Just when Jack thought he might keel over, he felt the fish relent. "Get the net!" he cried.

Carl reached into the water, netted the fish, and laid it on the deck between them. It was a lake trout, twelve or thirteen inches.

"That's the fish?" Jack said. He thought surely his overheated, dehydrated brain was hallucinating. "No way is that the fish."

"Critter put up a valiant battle."

"Hope we can all say the same when it's our time."

"Want a picture with you holding it?"

"I can hardly breathe."

"God, would you look at this?" Carl said. "Guys!" He opened his arms wide as if to encompass the boat, the lake, the starry canopy, the moon's gentle eye, and the men themselves within and a part of it all.

"So sweet," Billy agreed.

Jack only nodded, perspiring, a weary smile tenuous on his face. He was either fading into a calm, easy sleep . . . or dying. At the moment he didn't care which.

"Guess I ought to guide this vessel back to shore," Billy said.

Billy started the engine and raised the anchor. Jack was softly belching.

"What if the shore isn't there anymore?" Carl asked after a few minutes.

"Guess we'd get a lot more fishing in," Billy said.

"Look around," Carl continued. "We can't see land. Yet we assume that it's there."

Billy rearranged his crotch while steering with the other hand.

"I'm throwing this guy back in the water," Jack announced. He'd regained his composure. With grunting effort he stood, de-hooked the trout, and held it. A profound fishy odor ascended into his nose. He drew a breath to fill his lungs and then, with a loud battle cry, reached back and hucked the fish like he used to huck footballs back in the day. His coach used to tell him he had a pro-ball-type arm. The trout sailed out into the darkness so far that he couldn't hear the splash. For a few moments Jack stood facing the water, tears brimming.

The sun was a glowing orange line on the horizon as the *Huge Pen Is* reached the marina. Seagulls hovered along the beach, a light breeze caressed. Classic rock grooved on the radio. A perfect morning.

Pleasantly exhausted, sweaty, and slightly drunk, the men disembarked. Their flip-flops slapped against the dock as the gear-laden men made their way to their cars. Alone in the parking lot and miles from all responsibility, they embraced each other, promising to do this again really fucking soon.

Eve of Mania (Our Room)

Drew Buxton

OUR CYCLES WERE synced like periods.
We created together in our big room.
She hung her canvases everywhere,
I didn't need much space to write.

We'd feel it coming a few days before
but wouldn't say anything,
just chew on our cheeks and smile like kids
full of sugar.

On the eve of mania,
 it finding holes in our bad walls,
        we'd make that trip for coffee and
cigarettes,
the only things we craved.

Me writing and you painting over there,
No one knows what it's like in our room.

We created.

 She danced between canvases.

We fucked

and put down cigarettes like hammers to nails.

A roller coaster ride

of peaks and valleys.

Below deck,

to the cabin,

to wait out the turbulent waters.

Fuck that!

Because no one felt like us,

 and on the eve of mania,

in our big room,

we were free killers and no one was safe.

The Space Between

Ben Tanzer

I'm listening to X.

I'm in Los Angeles.

I am boxers, ice coffee, and sun and I am sweating my Los Angeles sweat, while I lay on my Los Angeles bed.

I am also running.

Always.

I run along 3rd Avenue this morning, past the Dash stops and the 7-Elevens, the people passing out religious tracts and motels more decrepit than mine, with their peeling sky-blue paint jobs, crappy little diners and shiny black Range Rovers.

As I stride down 3rd and up again I'm thinking about the space between.

For example, the space between now and the last time I wrote about running, or the relationship between running and balance and work when there is so much noise, but no clear route to follow.

Since my last running writing, I have run in Chicago, of course, but Boise, Ann Arbor and Baltimore as well, the latter just days ago. Should I have written about them?

Every four to five years I am asked to travel to Boise to speak at a conference. This year I discussed social norms and our efforts to understand the behavior of communities and the people in them, their misperceptions, and how exposing people to these gaps in understanding can infuse a community with positivity, transforming behavior, reducing social ills, and so on. All of which is cool stuff, narrowing the space between knowledge and reality to create change.

But what is also cool, is the trail there. Just steps from my room, it winds along the river behind the hotel.

It goes on for miles, and there are trees and cyclists, and over the years, more homes and buildings too, but it is still crisp and fresh, all crackly energy, flat, fast and peaceful. I look forward to the invitation to speak in Boise in part so I can go out there, unfettered, free and full of flow, my presence merely required in small jolts, my opportunities to run endless.

The Harbor in Baltimore is different, in all ways. It is about childhood and family and attending lectures at the school of social work just up the street. It is also about obligations, small children, drinks and meals, catching-up and hugs, squeezing time from wherever it will give, looking for chances to breathe and if everything goes mostly right, strapping on my running shoes for a moment of liberation.

And then there is Ann Arbor.

There are no true memories there, or real associations, not really, not yet. Nor am I there for work or family, but books and speaking, expenses paid, honorariums, and running when possible – and this is happening now, slowly, sometimes, this being asked to talk about being a writer, and it's exciting, like work, but not, because it's better, it's speaking about writing, words and craft.

It's a possible sort of future, even if I have no idea how to make it so.

I awake in my Los Angeles bed to calf cramps, something else that has been happening lately, and whether that is too much run and too little stretch, or lack of hydration, walking or shoes, the cramps are vise-like, the pain rippling, and I start the day by kneading my calves in the still dark room until they listen and then relax.

Yesterday, I got up early, packed my running gear and clothes for the day, and went down to Venice Beach.

Yogi Roth, a documentary filmmaker friend who created *Life in a Walk*, lives there, and the plan was to run and surf and eat burritos.

If I have been aspiring to any lifestyle goals beyond more writing, more flexible work days, and more money, it's creating this kind of morning – early run, surfing – something I haven't tried to do since I was teenager – tacos, or burritos, coffee, and then work, whatever that work is – the work of writing certainly, always, but podcasts, branding, and making change too – for me, for you, whomever.

It is also about the work that pays the bills though, always, if only I can just figure out how to mold my actual work life into something else, something more pliable and transformed.

Yogi and I take off to run along the beach, another trail, blue *Truman Show* skies going on forever, the waves and surf off in the distance; we talk, and I try to breathe, and I am going, one foot after another, and I think, this is real, it's happening, but yet not, not really.

I am in Los Angeles to attend a conference for writers.

It's on my own dime, as my father might say, my own vacation time, and there are no true obligations, except to do what I want.

And so it is that Yogi and I are now passing Santa Monica Pier, more childhood,

more memories, so many from so long ago
- Los Angeles in the 1980's, the girls, *The
Decline of Western Civilization*, *Blade
Runner*, and well, girls.

Soon we are back in the parking lot
where we started and we're stripping down,
pulling on wetsuits, grabbing surfboards
and heading to the ocean.

Yogi by the way is doing it - the
lifestyle thing.

He works like a motherfucker on his
day job, but he doesn't start until 10:00,
and before all of that, he's up early,
working out, eating well and making
documentaries and podcasts.

Is a life like this attainable for me
though?

I have thought it was Raymond
Pettibon's life I wanted - Southern
California artist, punk music, beach
community, cool shit.

And I do want that, badly, with every step, and breath.

But what if the life I am capable of having is actually more like Yogi's?

Cool shit, and art, always, and running, and tacos, and surfing, but working day jobs that pay, and pave, the way - plus teaching, hustling and transforming lives.

Or at least trying?

Maybe I have the model wrong?

When Yogi and I were still running, there was this moment where I was still able to talk, and Yogi mentioned the concept of the space between.

The space between is the space between hesitation and opportunity, how we can get stuck there and how we need to push past the hesitation and embrace the opportunities.

But how do we do that?

Since January I have been teaching, building out my website, crafting a series of handbooks, accepting invitations to participate in ever more literary events, and recording podcasts.

I have also been applying for jobs, even interviewing for one, but they have mostly been things I don't want.

Not that they necessarily want me.

And so there has been cool stuff, so much cool stuff. But opportunities to truly change my life? (My work life anyway?) No, not really.

Has there been hesitation?

Probably.

But in what ways?

I don't know.

We reach the ocean after stopping on the beach for Yogi to walk me through the steps: where my feet must be, and my hands. When I will jump to my feet, and how.

Even in a wet suit, the water is shocking at first, a slap, but I soon acclimate myself to it, it is fine, and there is new shit to worry about.

We begin to paddle out.

I cannot achieve any sort of balance on the board.

It's teetering.

I keep trying to focus, to not be scared and embrace it.

Yogi pushes me into a wave.

He tells me to go with it.

I glide, for just a moment, and it's exhilarating.

But then I can't do so again – I keep flipping over, the board repeatedly plunging forward and burying me in the surf.

Yogi suggests we step out, take a moment.

How's it going?

I can't stay balanced.

Head up, he says.

Try it.

You can do it.

Can I?

We go back-in.

I keep my head up.

I find balance.

I hit a wave and I go and go, and then again, and again, flying, gliding.

I'm ready to stand.

The first time I don't get beyond rising on my knees, but I ride the wave like that, and it is glorious.

Then more attempts, many more, the balance is happening.

More gliding, longer, amazing. I try to stand, I almost get there, but I stumble and tumble and pitch forward off of the front of the board.

Still, I am on a surfboard, it's real, as are the burritos we eat after we're done, the farmer's market and a feeling of being less.

This is not my normal day.

I am usually more, doing more – pushing, searching for things and reacting – and maybe if I'm going to achieve what I want I must be less, not more.

Opportunities are not always opportunities – saying yes to everything has not really been working for me, the life I have has not truly transformed into something else by doing so.

So, do less, live more?

As I head back up 3rd, sore calf, no sleep, the blue skies still everywhere and every which way, I think about the space between, hesitation, fear, and how much I've been wanting something else.

But maybe this is it. Running here, there and everywhere, and making friends and eating burritos, and surfing, and reading and writing and podcasting. Going to work, but also going out into the world and then coming home.

If I lift my head up and look around, focus, will I see I've already achieved some version of what I've wanted?

Should I step back, figure out what not to do, and stop fighting what I've already created?

Have I been chasing something I already have?

Can I figure out how to embrace it?

Jerry's Motel, Los Angeles, April 2016

Three Things to Reconsider

Matt Pine

Here are three things that you should reconsider. One: winter, early dark, a downtown street corner and Rachel at the top of the subway stairs. She is half-turned, waving at you and reaching for the banister with the same hand. Two: that seashell that reminds you of your mother. Three: Rachel (a different Rachel, a child, ten or eleven years old) standing beside you reading the teacher assignments—you will have the same homeroom for fifth grade.

That last thing is part of a ritual that I had assumed everyone shared, but writing it down I realized that it could have been regional, or perhaps not even. Perhaps it was unique to my elementary school. Every summer, one month before the first day of class, pieces of paper would appear taped to the school's front door. I remember them as computer printouts, the type with the perforated frills. These were the homeroom assignments. For each grade, there were exactly four teachers and approximately one hundred children. The methods used to assign homerooms were a secret, and therefore surrounded by speculation. (Was it truly random? Or were the rumors true, and certain families held a particular influence?) The kids in the school district sensed the approach of the announcement, in the same way birds know it's time to migrate. We would escape homes and babysitters and walk to school and look at the front door to see if the printouts had been posted. (Talking about this now, it sounds so Norman Rockwell, even though it was the 1980s in a not-so-safe bungalow suburb of Chicago.) We would check daily at first, and later, as the anticipation built, we would return hourly. And suddenly, they'd be up! And you'd find out if you had been stuck with a notorious witch, or if you'd be spending a year in the same class as your best friend. Or there were simpler concerns: in fifth grade my teacher's name was Ms. Blenz. I remember looking at her name and anticipating a year of writing the letter 'z,' and in a way that my adult brain can no longer feel, it made me happy.

As for the seashell, I recently spent a few minutes trying to find the name for it. Or I intended to only spend a few minutes, but I got lost. Seashells are the sort of natural phenomenon that sizzle the brain of analytic types. And analytic types are the sort that build an abundance of internet, so I found numerous catalogs with exacting details and subclassifications. I mean, pictures and pictures and pictures of seashells. When was last time you really looked at a seashell? The variety of shapes and colors makes fruit and vegetables look like variations on a narrow theme. Spikes and furls or arched and puckered, glassy or rough-hewn, flat or globular. You scroll down the page and you get millions of years of evolution condensed into one sweep of the eyes and all you can say is, "Whoa." Seashell names, on the other hand, are the type of words that writers use to make lazy, naturalist poetry: king's crown, lace murex, knobby whelk. The one that reminds me of my mother, it turns out, is called a 'junonia.' It has giraffe spots and a long, rippled opening that runs across it length-wise. The reason I associate it with my mother is that one sat on the jewelry try on her dresser for all of my childhood. There was the velvet box that held earrings, an empty bottle of perfume, a greasy powder case (my mom has never really worn makeup, so the same compact sat there for years), and that seashell. I had assumed she found it on a beach. That's how children think, isn't it? They go for the simple and common narrative? Well, here's something interesting that I just learned: junonia aren't typically found on the beach. Instead, they are dredged from the bottom of the sea and then sold in stores. Now it seems to me that the seashell must have been a gift, because my mom generally doesn't buy things for herself.

And Rachel, approaching the subway. We had been coworkers for two and a half years. In fact, we had started on the same day, which gave a cinematic twang to our...friendship? Well, we weren't exactly friends. We weren't exactly coworkers, even. We had worked in different departments, and nothing business-y ever involved both of us. At most, you could say that we were two employees of the same company who sporadically said 'Hi' to each other. That, and we shared another coincidence: our respective divorces had been finalized on the same day. This was strange, or at least unlikely, because I was thirty and she was thirty-one and neither of us were at all religious. That's what people mistakenly deduce when you get married young and there isn't a pregnancy involved (which is always their first guess, as if a baby reverts everything to 1950s morality and decorum). It takes a few volleys of questions and answers and questions and clarifications before someone really groks being young and in love and a complete moron. With Rachel and me, these double coincidences, they formed an inhibition-creation mechanism. We could not approach each other. Only the delusional try to touch the mirror, right?

And it wasn't just that you would get to see who was your teacher and who were your classmates, it's that you would get to take a look at them. There were a hundred kids in your grade—how had their faces changed? What whammies had biology worked on the body that summer? Some you had seen at the pool, some you had maybe had sleepovers with, but at a school of that size, there was a large cast of known strangers, kids whose faces and names and childhoods you knew and shared year after year while learning nothing about them and forming no intimacy. When you went to see your homeroom assignment, you would see teeth lost and teeth arrived, freckles baked in and freckles washed away, bones pushing out like poles stretching out a tent, new glasses, new clothes, new hobbies, new quirks, louder or rougher or shier or weirder, more boyish, more girlish, experimental traits, traumas buried and traumas sprouting, traumas giving fruit in savage little personalities. Fifth grade was the start of a wild bloom. After reading and admiring the name 'Blenz,' I noticed that Rachel was standing beside me.

And my dad, always the converse to my mother, had a bucket of seashells. He was an only child, and his parents, who were very poor, saved every artifact from his childhood. They had gone on precisely one family vacation, a road trip from Cincinnati to the Florida Keys. From what I understood, they arrived after a twenty-two-hour drive to discover that any motel they could afford was too sleazy to sleep in. They spent the night in the car. In the morning they went to the beach, where my child-aged dad had filled his pale with seashells. An hour later, they started the drive back. But his bucket of shells doesn't interest me. It's the junonia that you should reconsider.

And Rachel, coworker Rachel, well...what we had was a failure to have anything. Her desk was near the door, and maybe once a week I would stop and talk. We gave each other glimpses of our common difficulties. (Try explaining a twentysomething divorce on your first date. Too early, right? Okay, try explaining it on the fifth. Well, that's definitely too late. And no matter when you mention it, the way people react is completely unfair. It's muted. People think they're clever concealers, but they never are. You know what they're assuming, which is to say you make assumptions about their assumptions, and the whole conversation gets clogged up. You can for sure tell that they think you're hurt, and you wish they would ask questions so that you could clarify, but they never do, and there is no natural way for you to say that you are bold, that you are proud, and—fine, I'll confess—that you are in fact a little hurt. And no one, absolutely no one, thinks of it as what it was: a failed, but very earnest, but very failed, declaration of a romantic nature.) One Friday, after work, Rachel and I went to a party together, where we both got very, very drunk. At last, it seemed like the implied roles for us would finally get their audition that night, but for a moment we separated—to grab another beer, or refill a wine glass, or take a lap of the snack table—and she was cornered by a sheepishly muscular man. Does that phrase ring true in your head? Sheepishly muscular? You must have met someone like this before. He works in social justice, or something similarly admirable. He is very brainy and his talents could be very profitable if they weren't applied to a cause so noble. He might be a nonprofit lawyer, for example, or a Harvard business grad working in the developing world. He is strong, clean-shaven, with a very wide chest, arms stuffed with grapefruits, and a high-tension chevron for a neck. And he is sheepish, with poor posture, clumsy hands, hair that looks dry and meager. He is a mumbler. Well, one of those was talking to Rachel and I thought he looked happy, and I thought she looked happy, and so I left. Later, I heard he failed to even ask for her number.

And Rachel, the childhood one, she was looking for her homeroom assignment at the same time I was. I saw just how her face had changed. She saw how my face had changed. Puberty is a game where the cards are dealt face-up. You know where you both stand. You know the runs, you know the suites. You know what is hoped for and what is feared. You know when something long-wanted becomes impossible, and you see a long shot that hits its mark. You know when aspirations need to be moderated. You see resignation, or you see a failure of resignation. You see undeniable advantages, you see unfair luck in the envy-sense, you see unfair luck in the pity-sense. You see, however indirectly, what has changed about yourself, a self that had not yet, until it is observed by another person, been made real. And in that minute, looking at each other, what had grown in summer's secrecy was revealed. This is who we would be for that year, this is who we were becoming. We would take our adjustments together in Ms. Blenz's class.

And there is something that I want to ask my mother about that seashell, but I don't know how. I mean, I could call her. She is semi-retired, and I suspect, getting a little bored and a little lonely. But even if she were busy, she says that I never call enough and that she'd be glad to hear my voice. But it's not the significance to her that puzzles me. The seashell had kept me company in my childhood. It was a totem of mom-ness, and woman-ness, and lady-ness, and sitting as it was on my mother's jewelry tray, it was a marker of private ritual, and a hint that even in the most loving family relationship there would be an unknowable part. And perhaps that was enriching. And perhaps that was wonderful. It always made me happy to look at the seashell. By living in proximity to things we give them talents, which can be heightened or stripped away with interrogation. It is all outside of you, and you only wonder how to bring it in without destroying it.

And Rachel, descending into the subway. She had been laid off. It had been her last day in the office and we had, for the second time, gotten very, very drunk together. I had tried to put her into a cab, and she'd said that she was being frugal now. I had told her that I'd pay for it, but she had said why don't you just give me the money then and let me take the subway. It felt as unexpectedly bitter then as it does to type it now. But then, she had been laid off, and I had not, and somehow that put us on opposite teams. And so we parted outside the subway. We could have...Or, I could have...Or to be fair, she also could have...But no. Cleanly and concisely, we both made it clear that our time in each other's lives was concluding.

She waved, and I waved, and she walked down the stairs. And it was done. Another card had been dealt face-up. And now you know more now than you have ever known, and frankly, you are not at all wiser. The more that is revealed, the less you understand.

Dry City

Liz Yohe Moore

I.

MY LOVE FOR you sits torpid on the
kitchen floor
between dust and smashed plates

I have started stepping around it,
sometimes,
sweeping the circumference
dusting the top and sides

it is the most undeniable evidence
of what I have known all along

your ghost haunts this place:

the drape of afternoon sun on my bed

becomes your hair falling over one pillow,

the clattering of the cat in my (our)
bathroom
is the sound of your mascara and shadows

I occupy myself:

w h i l i n g
a   w   a   y

t
 h
  e

      h
         o
            u
               r
                s

the immutable imprint of your footstep
is fixed into the floor

invisible to guests:
to those who did not know you
and to those who did.

II.

once

walking down Sixth one muggy summer
night
Avenue of the Americas

God's image cast by the moon over the
Brooklyn Bridge

its penumbra a shadow of the baptismal
flame
roaring beneath a crank spoon

sweeping down to Williamsburg
society's scorned sleepers draped on
forgotten stoops

haunting disposable Internet cafes
on Avenue A one Sunday afternoon

windows folded open flooding with air
slim women with breeze-fluttered sleeves
bare legs looming large and sleek

hipster artistes clutching coffee
iBankers with sad smirks

free still:
untouched by your opiate eyes

III.

America you are the youth

swallowing cities in flashmobs
overflowing with puberty and exult

      impulse:
           revolution!

           evolution!

           confusion

           dissolution

In the summer discontent

explosive euphoria

R E L E A S E

THUNDERSHOCK

      sound vibrating

gunshots   or maybe fireworks?

I hit the ground in ignorance

you and I hadn't met yet

this was a different life

it was not the same me

IV.

sweet kids in Union Square beckon me beyond

they dance with rumpled canvas pants

crowned by immaculate dreads

painted with inarticulate beliefs

dreaming of Wall Street days

endless summer nights
exhilarate with echoes
blossoms passed into fodder

flagrant nights of dancing, sometimes
stepping on the feet of humanity
coltish birth into rhythm, all of us

moving as though shoes of fire
had been sorcelled to our feet

4am train rocking back and forth
crawl dragging through the
manicured Central Park stations
hitting
every
stop
with finality.

Through to Harlem

maybe someday someway finally: home

the Heights

jubilant drums insistent

Dominican teens powered

by the flush of youth

and celebration of good company

youth belongs to sound

even at 4am

over the drums, across the aisle

you are sitting rumpled and tired

bag drooping into the neighboring seat

waving off advances with a polite smile

when our eyes meet

they speak languages unknowable by the
tongue

Homefront

Giano Cromley

At 10:17 AM Monty got the call informing him that his mother had died sometime the day before. She'd passed away in the home. Luckily, a worried neighbor had called in an anonymous wellness check. Otherwise...well, Monty didn't want to think about otherwise. He'd always known this day would come, that he'd be compelled to go back. Better to do it quickly, he thought. One last clean break.

Maura wanted him to wait, at least until their son's fever broke. They'd argued about it. One of those trench warfare fights they'd been having lately where they were both so dug in neither of them seemed to have a way of communicating, much less surrendering. When it was over, he booked the next available flight. That afternoon, looking down on the clouds as his plane climbed away from Chicago, Monty realized what he'd been unable to tell Maura: He needed to go back alone.

....

The old phone in his mother's kitchen let out a grinding ring that shattered the quiet of the empty house. Monty stared at it. He felt vulnerable, an intruder caught behind enemy lines.

"Jesus, Monty, where have you been?" It was Maura. "Your phone's going straight to voicemail."

He could hear a faint cry on the other end. Sounded like Caitlin - just part of the white noise that permeated their daily existence.

"Is everything okay with Dillon?" he asked.

"Same. Fever hasn't broken."

"And the doctor?"

"Said to wait."

The line was quiet. All essential information had been exchanged.

"I must've forgotten to turn my phone on after the plane," he said. "Sorry."

There was a slight pause in Caitlin's crying. Maura asked, "What's it like being back?"

"Pretty depressing so far." There was more he could say but didn't, perhaps to protect her from the true darkness of his mood.

"Any regrets?"

Monty wasn't sure if she was fishing for an apology. "Of course," he said. "I have regrets about almost everything." He could hear how bad this sounded as soon as the words left his mouth, so he added, "I wish you could be here."

This last line was bait, he supposed, to let Maura reignite their earlier argument. She sighed instead, a semaphore of resignation.

"Forget it," he said. "Let me know if things change with Dillon."

"Keep your phone on," she said. "I can't believe I still had your mom's number in my contacts."

When he hung up, the house fell silent. It was dark outside, only a fraction brighter inside. His two main responsibilities were arranging some kind of memorial service for his mother and settling the estate. Both tasks would be easier to accomplish if he could get a hold of his brother Simon. There'd been no answer when he'd tried reaching him earlier. It would be just like Simon to dodge this final obligation.

Monty opened his cell phone and pulled up the most recent number he had for his brother. Instead of hitting send, though, Monty decided to dial from his mother's phone. Between the first and second rings someone picked up.

"I'm trying to reach Simon Creel," he said.

"Are you joking?" The voice belonged to a woman – young, sullen.

"This is the last number I have for him," Monty said. "Simon's my brother. Our mother has died."

"This isn't his number anymore." Her voice was harder now, as if the fact that their mother was dead had made her less sympathetic.

"Do you know where I can reach him?" Monty asked, but she'd already hung up.

....

It was 6:45 AM when he awoke. It had been a restless sleep. At one point, on the edge of consciousness, he could have sworn he'd heard footsteps, the same sound his father used to make when he'd stagger down the hallway at night. But now Monty wasn't sure if it had been a dream. Ghosts, he knew, were nothing more than powerful memories. And there were plenty of those to go around.

He went through the house opening shades and windows. The estate sale people would arrive in a couple hours. This was a little rushed, a breach of etiquette perhaps, but he wasn't about to stand on ceremony.

His mother hadn't done much to keep things up the last couple years. Stacks of newspapers circling the dining room; mugs with dried rings of coffee measuring daily evaporation rates. The sorry sight of it would have induced a better man to feel guilty, but it just made Monty lonely. He tried calling Maura. He wanted to tell her that nothing from the past, neither these rooms nor his memories of them, seemed like they were the right size anymore. The phone rolled over to voicemail so he hung up.

He found some cleaning supplies under the sink, then turned on the kitchen radio. The work was gratifying. The ammonia fumes scalded his nostrils as bucket after bucket became cloudy, then brown, from years of accumulated dirt. He was bringing this house back to an earlier time.

As he was running a vacuum through the bedroom he'd shared with Simon, a nostalgic memory came back. He knelt down, counted ten floorboards from the foot of the bunk beds, and knocked until he found a hollow spot. Using his thumbnail, he pried up the loose board to find the cubbyhole where he'd kept his adolescent stash of *Playboys* and *Penthouses*. They were gone. In their place, he found a Ziploc bag.

Monty picked it up, held it to the light. A couple joints, some white pills, several folded squares of foil, and a key that looked like it might fit a bus station locker. Fucking Simon. Monty shoved the bag into his pocket. He heard his cell phone ring back in the living room but it stopped by the time he got there. Maura. He listened to the message. No change with Dillon.

....

Afternoon found Monty dragging a stack of newspapers through the front door, mentally calculating how many would fit into the trunk of his rental car. All at once, he had a feeling he was being watched.

A man stood on the sidewalk wearing a heavy flannel shirt and dirty work boots. His head was pear-shaped, with large black glasses.

Monty figured it was one of his mother's friends who wanted to offer his condolences. He gave the stranger a sad smile and tried to slide the stack with his feet while holding the screen door open.

It'd be a lot easier to throw the papers out, but Maura was a merciless recycler and the habit had worn off on him.

When he looked up again, the man was still standing on the sidewalk, watching.

"Monty Creel?" he said. "Is that you?"

"Hi, hello," Monty said, trying to strike the right balance between familiarity and fuck-off.

"Carl Nelson," the man said. "Roosevelt High. Class of '94."

"Carl Nelson," Monty said, summoning astonishment. They'd probably exchanged all of ten words with each other in high school. Different circles – a Venn diagram with almost no overlap.

"Hey," Carl offered, "you remember that time we ditched Mr. Dolan's P.E. class and went to Tom McKay's house to smoke one of his dad's cigars?"

Monty was certain the memory belonged to someone else, but he smiled and nodded politely. Carl began walking across the lawn, killing any hope Monty had of keeping the encounter brief.

"I was just cleaning up," Monty said.

"I heard." Carl perched a foot on the first porch stair. "Can't tell you how sorry I am." His voice clenched. His eyes were red and rimming. This stranger felt worse about Monty's mother than Monty did.

"Thanks. That means a lot."

"I heard it happened right inside there." Carl stepped up onto the porch and peered in.

"That's what they told me."

"Life, man. So fragile, isn't it?" He bit his lip and lowered his head. He stood there, unmoving.

Monty wasn't sure what to do. "Did you want to come in for a minute?" he offered.

Carl stepped over the threshold and into the living room. He sat down on the couch and propped his work boots on the coffee table. The glass top looked like it might shatter under the weight.

"I've been out of touch for a while, Carl. Did you know my mother?"

Carl looked at the walls on either side of the room. Something about his face had changed in the last few seconds. "Not really," he said. "I do know your brother pretty well, though."

Monty felt a sharp tingle shoot through his fingertips.

"I probably don't have to tell you Simon isn't the most reliable person in the world," Carl said. "He was supposed to leave something for me. There should've been a key."

The two men faced each other across the living room. Neither of them spoke. The moment took on physical properties – density, mass, boundaries. Monty knew there was a simple way to end this standoff: give this guy the Ziploc bag and be done with it. There was no reason it had to go on a minute longer. But an anger had been ignited in him and he wasn't ready to let it go out.

"I know what you're looking for," Monty said. "It's gone. I threw it away this morning, with the first load of garbage I took to the dump."

Carl's nostrils flared. "If you're telling me the truth, that's going to be a problem."

The doorbell rang. Carl's eyes cut to the front of the house.

"Hold on," Monty said.

When he opened the door, he saw a thin woman with gray hair pulled back in an efficient-looking ponytail. "Mr. Creel, I'm Sandy Jenkins. We spoke yesterday about the estate." Her voice struck a note of practiced gravity. "Is now a good time to get started?"

Behind her was a short man with the build of a bear, and a clipboard in one hand. "Um," Monty said, "why not?" He opened the door to let them in. "The place is kind of a mess. I'd hoped to have it in better shape."

The pair looked around, instantly assessing.

When Monty turned back to the living room, Carl was gone. He heard the sound of the back door closing quietly. Monty raced to the kitchen and looked out the window just in time to see Carl slip through the back gate.

"Mr. Creel," Sandy Jenkins called, "are you there? Shall we get started?"

"I'm sorry," he said, returning to the living room. "So how does this work?"

"It's up to you," she said. "We understand there's a lot of emotions at a time like this. Obviously there's things you'll want to keep, for sentimental reasons. You can be involved in this process as much as you'd like."

Monty looked around the house, at the faded prints on the walls, the fake ferns hanging in the window. He could not summon one good memory of this place.

"Sell everything you can," he said. "Throw the rest away."

....

"Where are you?" he asked.

There was a moaning sound on the other end. "Emergency room," Maura said. "Dillon's fever spiked. Doctor said to bring him in."

Monty's hand clenched the steering wheel. "What are they saying?"

"We've been waiting over an hour and no one's seen him yet."

"What?" He'd been driving around aimlessly since leaving the estate sale people at his mother's house. Now he pulled over to the side of the road.

"This place is a shit-show," Maura said. "A fucking disaster."

Sitting in his rental car alone, Monty felt worse than helpless – he felt responsible.

"Let me talk to someone," he said.

"No, Monty."

"Put me on with someone. Give the phone to whoever's in charge."

He could hear her talking.

Then: "Hello." It was a woman's voice, at once officious and desultory.

"Do you have any idea how long my son has been waiting to see someone?"

"Sir, I'm not—"

"He needs medical attention."

"We have a lot of sick people that need attention, sir."

"I don't care how many people there are. Only one of them is my son."

"If you were here you'd see how busy we are."

Monty's ears began to buzz. "Do you understand what it means to suffer?" he whispered.

"Excuse me?" she said.

"One of these days," he said to the woman, "someone's going to show you what pain really is."

He heard the line click. The buzzing in his ears receded. He waited ten minutes for Maura to call him back. When she didn't, he texted: "Sorry."

....

The sign out front said "Shooters Tavern." He'd never been here before, but he knew this area of town. It was an industrial corridor, south of the frontage road.

Monty parked the car on the street and went in. The place was as big and welcoming as a bus terminal, so new it smelled more like a construction site than a club. It wasn't late, but the place was snarled with people, starting at the bar and stretching to the far walls. There was a stage to the rear set up for a band.

Monty took a position against the wall. It was a baggy pants and baseball cap crowd. He was easily the oldest person here.

"What are you drinking?" A cocktail waitress with a trim body balanced a serving tray on one hand.

"Whiskey and soda," Monty said.

She eyeballed him. This was not the kind of place for that drink, but he knew he'd look more foolish if he switched, so he nodded and went back to scanning the room.

Monty knew he'd come here because it was the type of bar Simon might frequent. But he was less certain why he was bothering to look for him at all. Spite? Anger? Probably. Or maybe he was here simply to find out why he still felt the need to see him.

"Four bucks." The waitress was back. How she managed to surf her way through this thicket of people with a tray of drinks was beyond Monty.

He pulled out a ten and gave it to her, nodded to keep the change. He drank until the ice slid against his nose. A trickle of perspiration ran down his spine.

When the band walked on stage, the crowd instinctively moved towards it, iron filings drawn to a magnet. Then he glimpsed a face he recognized. It had been four years, but he still saw something he knew in that face: himself, only thinner, paler, older.

A moment later, the band buzzed to life – whining guitars; mumbled, inaudible lyrics. Simon was watching the band but didn't seem to be enjoying himself, wasn't swaying or patting his chest the way everyone else was.

Monty allowed himself to edge closer until he stood right behind his brother. He leaned over his shoulder and spoke.

"I found the bag you hid in the bedroom." Monty wasn't sure why this was the first thing he said to his brother after so much time, but he knew immediately it was a poor choice.

Simon didn't move for a few seconds. Then he bolted – threading and shoving his way toward an emergency exit. It wasn't until Simon had nearly made it to the door that Monty decided to give chase.

The air was cold outside. He was in some kind of alley and he just caught sight of his brother as he cut around the edge of the building.

"Simon!" he called out after him.

But Simon was already gone. When Monty reached the front, he saw his brother running down the center of the street. Then, perhaps realizing how exposed he was, Simon veered off the road and threw himself at a chainlink fence.

Monty reached him before he could scramble over. He grabbed his shirt and yanked him down. Simon fell into a heap in the gravel.

"You fucking idiot!" Monty yelled, standing over him.

Simon looked woozy. His head lolled, and his hair hung in a curtain over his eyes.

"Why are you running from me?"

"Isn't it obvious?" Simon asked.

"I wanted to see you."

"Why? So you could feel superior?" Simon's voice was raspy. "I hope you're not disappointed."

"I can't say I'm surprised." A train whistle blew somewhere in the near distance. A shaky roar began to vibrate the ground. "Mom's dead. Did you even know that?"

"I need the key," Simon said. "The one in the bag. You can keep the rest but I need that key."

"Did you hear me? She's dead."

Simon started to pick himself up off the gravel. "I know," he said. "I was there."

"You were?" The train was loud now and still growing.

"Of course I was. I was there when she died and I stayed with her until the paramedics showed up."

"But why—" The train's roar was so ferocious now there was no point talking, and the question – whatever it was – didn't seem worth asking once it had passed.

"I'm not really popular with the local authorities," Simon said. "But you probably could've guessed that."

"What's wrong with you?" Monty asked.

Simon shook his head. "This place, this town, it maims you. It doesn't even have the decency to kill you."

Monty knew this was the best answer his brother could give. "Forget I asked," he said. "All I want is help with mom. We have responsibilities."

at his phone. Four missed calls, all of them from Maura. He hit send.

After the third ring, he prepared himself for voicemail, but when the line stopped ringing it was her. In one word, *Hello,* he could feel the tiredness in her voice – exhausted from all she'd gone through with the kids, the fever, the emergency room. The sound stung him. He started crying, lightly at first, but it grew until his whole body was shaking.

"What's the matter?" she asked, her voice suddenly alert, tender.

He couldn't answer right away.

"Monty," she said, "what's wrong? Tell me."

He forced himself to catch his breath, to be still. The line was so clear it made the distance between them seem like nothing. He could sense her body heat, her pulse, through the phone.

"I need you," he said. "I need you with me."

She didn't say anything for a few moments. And the silence was so perfect and deep he could almost imagine what her next words would be.

time travelers

Chris Reid

MAYBE IT'S STILL not too late
    to unscrew you
to de-ejaculate your manhood
    withdrawing
as i primly close my thighs

standing by the headboard
    we would dress each other
i'd fasten your shirt from the bottom up
    you'd reclasp my bra with one hand
retreating down the corridor
    we would draw apart

settled at the kitchen table
    before matching coffee mugs
we'd be just another two people
    who'd never been intimate together

and the sheets on my bed
would not carry your scent

Buried in the Snow

Traci Failla

I watched my mother wrap her hands around her coffee cup and stare at the heavy snowflakes through the picture window in her kitchen. Adorned only by the small, ruffled valiance that hung above, it framed my childhood backyard like an oversized snapshot that changed with the seasons. I sat at an angle, watching her reflection cast against the cascade of white outside.

After three years of not hearing from my brother, Rocky, her third child, she began to pause more when it snowed, as if she were looking for an answer to some question in the flurries.

Rocky had loved the snow. It seemed like the only thing that had made him happy as a kid. On a day like this, he'd race home from school, dive into his snow gear, and dash out the back door as quickly as he had entered. He never wore a hat, and my mother would call to him every five minutes to put one on.

"My head needs to feel this snow, Mom," he said. None of us understood what he meant, but his voice was genuine enough that we knew it wasn't his usual defiance.

I never joined Rocky in the back yard. I was the oldest child of three, and in contrast to his status as the youngest, had plenty of indoor responsibilities. When it snowed, I was happy to have all these duties. I could avoid snow when it fell back in those days, but I never completely escaped it. Here I was in my mom's kitchen, still.

Rocky did though. He was somewhere in Memphis, Tennessee. At least that's where he had been the last time anyone heard from him.

Memphis was supposed to be his "new hometown," a term that we imagined brought relief to him but the pain of rejection to my mother. Though the move was described as a chance to start his life over, and with all the enthusiasm the thought of a clean slate elicited from eternally hopeful types, none of us believed it would give him what he needed.

Days like this worried my mom. Most of the time, she could push Rocky's absence out of her mind. These little bits of frozen precipitation were like kamikazes to her, plummeting to the ground with no regard for anything around them. She believed that Rocky was doing the same thing.

"He's a reckless boy," she said, cracking the silence. We hadn't been talking about him, but I knew what she meant.

"Mom, maybe he's okay. Maybe he's grown up. He's 31 now, after all." This was my standard line of comfort that we both knew was implausible. Rocky had never been okay. No one expected Rocky to ever grow up.

"Lisa, will you go down to Memphis and look for him?"

Our mother had never asked my middle brother, Steve, or I to do such a thing, though we often braced ourselves when his name came up. She knew that Rocky's departure had lifted an intense burden on the rest of us. We didn't wish him harm, but it was so much easier for us to not know what he was doing, not endure his requests for money, not visit him in the police station at 3:30 a.m. only to find out that the $100 we brought wouldn't cover his bail.

I looked out the window, watching the snow fall with the familiar sense of disappointment. I wasn't sure how to say no.

"I know this is a lot to ask of you," my mother said, "and I wish I could be the one to do this, but I need to stay here for Sasha."

Sasha was Rocky's daughter, now under the guardianship of my mother. How this came to be was typical of Rocky's life. An impressionable and emotionally fragile young lady fell in love with him. Her parents had died in a car accident the year before, and she found comfort in their relationship and, especially, the presence of my mother. But the toll of being a young mother, essentially orphaned and unmarried, was too much for her. When she fell off a bridge, the story was that she was drunk and messing around, being risky. No one wanted to suggest that her circumstances were too overwhelming.

"If you really want to do this, Sasha could stay with us while you go to Memphis," I said.

"I can't do that." Her face was drained. Dark circles imposed on the beautiful blue that only Rocky shared with her. "It's going to involve cell phones and the Internet. You know I'm not good with technology."

I pressed my lips together to retain my next suggestion. She could hire a private detective. But I knew that it was too embarrassing for her to bring in a stranger. I licked my top lip and sighed, drawing in air like it was the courage I needed to say yes or no to this request.

I heard Sasha turn on the television in the next room. My brother gave us one of the most beautiful children in our family. She was sweet too, which we all attributed to her mother. I wished we had known her mother better. If she were still alive, it would be one less mess Rocky left behind.

Sasha ended up in my mother's custody before Rocky left for Memphis. It didn't take much to convince him that our mother would be a better guardian than he would a parent, and I didn't give up hope that he signed those papers because he wanted Sasha to have the best shot he could give. The irony is that he never thrived under my mother's care, no matter how hard she tried.

It always amazed me at how Rocky managed to find new paths for himself. Six months after our mother adopted Sasha, he left. He said he was managing his friend's blues band, and Memphis was the place for their big break. But his friend never left his job up here, and Rocky never returned.

After a few months he stopped calling and texting. We assumed his cell phone service was cut off. He had a history of inconsistent employment and hadn't always paid his bills. My mother worried that something worse had happened. I just didn't want to think about it

....

Friday morning at five o'clock, I switched on the radio in my car and listened to the traffic report. I picked up the piece of paper on the passenger seat where I had written the last address we had for him—the last clue to Rocky's whereabouts.

I pulled out of the garage and drove past the ample homes and lovely yards that were my cocoon. I did not want to do this. I regretted this the moment my alarm went off this morning. Yet, I couldn't back out on this commitment and break my mom's heart for the thousandth time. Only, it would be my first time. Rocky had already broken it 999.

Eight hours later, I parked in front of a dilapidated mansion that had been chopped up into questionably legal housing. I considered that perhaps Rocky was here and that this would be easier than I thought. I walked to the front door, snagging my slacks on thistle weeds that pushed onto the scraggly sidewalk. There were seven different buzzers to press. None of the names appeared to be Rocky's, but most were faded so it was hard to be certain.

I pressed the only button that had a clear name on it. I was about to turn back to my car when the door cracked open.

"Yeah?" said a shirtless, long-haired guy who reminded me of Matt Dillon's character from the movie *Singles*.

"Hi," I responded. "My name is Lisa Wallis. My brother Rocky Quinn lived here a while back. Maybe he still does. This is the last address we have for him."

"Rocky?" he said. "What kind of a name is that?"

Before I could respond, he turned his head back over his shoulder and yelled, "Johnson! You know any guy named Rocky?"

I heard footsteps approach the door, and a guy in the Grateful Dead t-shirt with a blond ponytail pulled it open further.

"Who are you?" he said.

I explained my situation again. His eyes narrowed for a moment, then he said, "Yeah, I see the resemblance. In your nose."

The dark-haired guy nodded.

"So you know my brother?" I was amazed to have made this much progress so soon.

"Yeah, he owes me money." He brushed a few crumbs off the front of his shirt and winked. "But I'll let that slide."

"Do you know where he is?"

"If I did, he wouldn't owe me money anymore," he said. "But I do have a number from someone else who's looking for him. Hold on."

The blond went back into his apartment while the dark-haired guy made small talk about the weather. I got the sense that he felt sorry for me.

"Here," Mr. Grateful Dead said as he handed me the card.

Alan White

Detective

Memphis Police Department

"A police office," I said, unsurprised. "What does he have to do with my brother?"

"It must have been a long time since you've known your brother," he said.

I opened my bag and put the card in my wallet, avoiding his face. "Thanks for the help."

In the car, I sat for several minutes with my key in the ignition, staring at the card. I did know my brother, and I understood that any involvement he had with the police likely wasn't innocent. I didn't want to raise any red flags by bringing attention to him with this officer. But, I had come all this way and made a promise to my mother.

Dread tainted the rest of the afternoon. Walking up and down Beale Street didn't feel right. I lingered over the boredom of having nothing else pressing to do and the anticipation of not wanting to do what was pressing.

I had an early dinner at the hotel, twirling each strand of spaghetti, stretching the minutes out as long as I could. When I decided to phone Detective

White, my hope was that he had plans and wasn't prepared to interrupt them for a call.

Back in my hotel room overlooking downtown, I wondered if my brother was even still here. I felt like an intruder. I had a sense that Rocky slept on floors of other people's apartments while I had the comparative luxury of staying in his town in one of the nicest hotels in the city. It was unfair of me to come here like this. Rocky was a grown man and in charge of his own life, despite how much we didn't approve of it.

Oh, God, just get it over with, I thought. You know you need to do this.

I picked up the phone and dialed the detective. After two rings, he answered.

"Detective White." His voice was calm and reassuring, and I felt relief for my brother that he was being tracked by someone who might be sympathetic.

....

Two days later, I sat in a coffee shop that was drowning in silence. I had waited 25 minutes for Rocky to show up.

Rocky sat across from me at the small table, scooting backward and forward in his seat as if he were trying out which position would be the most comfortable, not yet finding it. He was smaller than I remembered, probably due to weight loss, but he still reminded me of a man sitting in a little preschooler chair at a parent-teacher conference, so out of place, so wrong for his environment.

"I don't drink coffee," he said. I wondered if this was an excuse for not having any money to buy himself a drink.

"They have other things here," I told him, "What do you like? I'll see if they have it."

"I don't need anything."

As I approached the counter under the pretense of getting another for myself, I backtracked to our childhood, trying to remember what Rocky liked and the snowy scenes from our back yard.

I sat a cup down at the table. "I thought you might want a hot chocolate since you don't get too many snow days down here."

He looked up, worried, and then thanked me.

He wrapped his hands around the cup but didn't drink. I wondered if he was cold, if he spent too much time outside.

Trying not to be obvious, I observed his clothes, hair, and face. He hadn't had a haircut in a while. His curls hung in spirals along the back of his neck like they did in late August before our annual back-to-school rituals. Mom always used to say, "Rocky's starting to look like Robert Plant. Time for haircuts!"

I thought about bringing it up, but forced the words back from the front of my mouth. I wasn't sure if memories of childhood were a reprieve from his current troubles or a painful reminder that life would probably never be as innocent as it was then.

He was closely shaven, though, and his clothes were reasonably clean and in decent condition. He wore a pair of jeans and a red thermal shirt with a Members Only jacket over it. I assumed the jacket was from the Salvation Army or something like that. I didn't think he was being ironic and retro.

"So, you're in town visiting a friend?" he asked. I couldn't tell if he was doubtful or just trying to make conversation.

"I am. She's an old colleague from work. She just had a baby, which is why I'm not staying with her. You know, that would be too much to ask." I was babbling like a classic liar.

"Hmmm." He stared past me, pretending to take an interest in the staff cleaning the espresso machine. Finally, he sipped his hot chocolate. I wanted that first sip to bring back home, but when he set the cup down, we were still in Memphis. I was still sitting across the table from my grown brother who ran away from us and never looked back.

"Do you miss the snow?" I asked Rocky, meaning did he miss us, did he miss Mom, did he miss his old life. Of course, I knew he didn't. But maybe he did miss the snow.

"Yeah," he said, "I do. But warmer weather is much more convenient to get around in. And I'm a pretty busy guy."

Detective White had told me a little about how Rocky had been spending his time in Memphis. Fortunately he wasn't in trouble with the police...not yet, anyway. He was involved with a woman who was a key witness in a drug trafficking trial. This didn't mean he was innocent, the detective cautioned, but it did mean that he wasn't directly tied to this case.

"So the band thing," I said, "it didn't work out?"

"Naw," said Rocky. "Those guys never had the guts to leave their day jobs and come down here. I heard that they aren't even playing at O'Leary's anymore. It's a shame. We could have really gone somewhere down here."

Rocky straightened his shoulders and lifted his chin. I did everything I could to look like I bought his story.

"Mom says you don't call," I said.

"I got screwed over by the phone company. They say I owe them money for some calls that I never made. I told them to go to hell." He chuckled, "I guess they don't need my business. They have plenty of other gullible customers to rip off."

"So you don't have a phone?"

"Naw. Who needs a phone anyway? I have a good network of associates. I don't need to be tracked down by some phone company that just wants to take what's not theirs."

I nodded, wishing I could relate more, or be more relatable. Why did he have to use the word *associates*? It was something I would need to spin for my mom, unless I wanted to be honest with her. I hadn't decided yet if I would be.

I began to time the pauses on the clock on the wall just to the right of

Rocky's head. Everything was calculated now, like a game of chess that neither of us would win. We would only endure it until our time was up, and we could go our separate ways.

The clock showed that he had been there for 15 minutes. How much longer would I force him to endure my presence? I imagined his discomfort and was thankful that he even came in the first place. This visit fulfilled my obligation, as unsatisfying as it ended up being. We had barely made a connection.

"Well, I'm sure you're busy," I said, guilt nudging me as I thought about how little I had probed. "Do you have an address where we can reach you?"

I gave him no time to answer. "Here's my card, if you ever need anything."

He patted the pocket of his jacket. "I must have left my cards somewhere."

"That's okay," I said, handing him a pen and another card, not sure if he was mocking me or just trying too hard. "Just put your info on the back of this one."

"I'm kind of between places right now," he said, holding the pen in mid-air above the back of my card. "I'm staying at my friend Mike's, but by the time you get back north, I'll be someplace else." He looked up with a smile. "I'll write you when I get settled, okay?"

"Sounds like a plan," I said, standing from the table to attempt a hug.

Before I could reach him, he asked, "How's Sasha?"

Now guilt stabbed me. It hadn't even occurred to me that he'd be curious about his daughter.

"Sasha! Of course! Here, take this. It's her picture."

Rocky held the photo by its edges. I had laminated it before I came down, thinking it would travel better in his pocket with some protection. He stared at it for a long time. When he finally took a deep breath, he sniffled. He looked at me with red-rimmed eyes.

"Sorry," he said. "Allergy season comes early in Memphis. Can I keep this?"

"I wanted you to have it. She's doing great. Everyone loves her."

"Thanks," he said, as he wrapped his arms around my neck. I held him long enough for the feeling to burn into my memory. I wished I could have boxed up that hug and brought it home to my mother.

"Gotta go." He walked out of the coffee shop, a little more bouncy than when he had come in.

....

Five months later I was in Memphis again, in the same hotel and even the same room. This geographic congruity contrasted the drastic difference between the purpose of my first visit and that of my second.

Rocky had never called or written. No one had expected him to, not even our mother. I decided to be honest with her about his situation and our conversation, agonizing if I had made the right decision, until I received last week's call from Detective White.

A couple of officers who worked with White had discovered Rocky lying on a pile of old clothes behind a vacant building, an empty bottle of whiskey at his fingertips. It was too late. He had been dead for an hour or so.

White explained that it was likely alcohol poisoning, or complications from hepatitis, or both. It had taken only a few seconds to decide that the cause didn't matter. We had hoped that Rocky's trajectory was calibrated toward something better. Instead he died behind a building somewhere too far for us to help. He was, in life and death, always out of reach.

All my mother said was, "Please bring my baby boy home."

Whether he liked it or not, I had come to get him.

I looked out over the city. The streetlights were on, but the sun was still high. Only a few people moved on the sidewalks. Hot and humid July drove them into the air conditioning.

I circled through the room picking up the bath gel, flipping through the movie guide, fingering the thick towels like an automaton. I wrapped my hands around my upper arms. The frigid air seeped from the walls, bestowing a complete absence of warmth. I didn't need the A/C right now. I was cold enough on the inside.

My mind was infected with the image from the afternoon, watching them pull out the drawer, looking down at Rocky's face. They had his childhood dental records, but I felt responsible for confirming this for my family, and to take the edge off his dying so alone. At least someone would visit him.

I didn't want to send his body home like that. My mother hadn't seen him since before he left for Memphis. She didn't know Rocky with a scruffy beard, tangled hair, and yellowed face. But she needed to see him to know on a more-than-conscious, informational level that this was real. So I made arrangements for his body to arrive as soon as possible back home. We had already planned for cremation and a memorial service. She would at least get the chance for a one-sided goodbye.

I left the room to melt the coldness that made my emotions inaccessible. Memphis was where Rocky thought he was going to change his fortunes. If I could feel what it was about this place that attracted him, maybe I would be able to better represent to my mother what had happened.

As I walked into the elevator, I dropped my room card into my pocket, and heard paper crinkle. I pulled out the map of Memphis I had used to find my way to the morgue. White had been there. He had shown me where Rocky was found. The building was only six blocks or so from my hotel.

I guessed that the neighborhood probably wasn't one of the city's finest, but the few blocks that lie before me in that direction appeared more sparse than rough. If there seemed to be trouble, I could always turn around.

Beyond my hotel, I passed the FedEx Forum and started toward the area beyond it. There were no houses along the way. A church turned golden in the setting sun, standing tall and proud. A block or two later the buildings progressed from new and pristine to marginally disheveled. Smooth concrete gave way to sidewalks marked with weeds and cracks. I began to see graffiti on the walls. Wrought-iron fences disappeared, replaced by chain link.

I reached the intersection where they found Rocky and saw a large brick building painted in two shades of violet. I looked at the map in my hands. That was the place. Across the way were a collection of brick apartment buildings that bore the hints of public housing with their stained roofs and repetitive design. They were tidy, though, and the area felt safer than I expected.

The windows of the purple building were boarded up. Signs from businesses previously there still hung above the multiple doors that were situated along the street side. Rocky's body had been found at the back of the building.

I had imagined it as a dank spot populated with heaps of substance abusers passed out on top of dirty third-hand sleeping bags around a small fire tended by a half-conscious sentry. But in this evening hour with the sun only just fading, I saw two kids who looked to be about high school age in a tête-à-tête over a cigarette, sucking it down like it was the breath of life. There was a plaid blanket stuffed behind some boards that leaned up against the back entrance. Weed trees grew from gaps in the concrete of what must have been a driveway or loading area. A brief gust of wind disturbed the dirt and then died back.

I ran my fingertips along the bottom edge of my sunglasses to wipe the perspiration from my cheekbones. There were no tears. This locale drew nothing from me. My sadness didn't belong here; it belonged at home. The man who died here was not the one I mourned. It was the boy inside who was never really prepared for this world, who never managed to find his peace in it.

....

Nearly six months after Rocky died, his ashes remained in an urn on top of my mother's dining room credenza. She was not a church-goer, but each time she walked by she'd cross herself or say a prayer.

She reserved the dining room for special occasions, but the presence of the urn made dinners there impossible. The room had turned into a mausoleum for her baby boy.

When we gathered that Christmas Eve, we started a new tradition. Instead of the dining room, we ate in the great room around the big screen watching a slide show of old family photos, many of Rocky. "It's for Sasha," my mom said. "I want her to feel connected."

Though it was not our habit, we stayed overnight to open gifts the next morning. No one had to say that it was because of Rocky. It turned out to be convenient. That night a snowstorm buried the town with twelve inches in six hours, and few plows were out on the holiday.

I went to bed in Rocky's old room with a sense of unfinished business. Scanning the ceiling, I checked off the gifts and the Christmas cards and the grocery list in my head. Sleep took over before I willed the feeling away.

Around 3 a.m., I heard a loud thud that sounded like a snowball hitting the window. Before I opened my eyes, I felt the sensation of Rocky's arms around my neck, reliving that last hug in Memphis.

Another lump of snow hit the sliding glass doors to our backyard, and I went downstairs to watch it pile up in the yard. On my way, I was drawn to the dining room, to the urn. It was all so automatic.

As I picked it up, I recalled hearing something about how there are sometimes pieces of bone in the ashes. Something knocked against the side as I shook it. I reached in and sifted through the soft dust. I pulled out a jagged piece of what I decided was a bone.

The snow was as deep as a mattress in the backyard. In my flannel pajamas, no boots, no gloves, no hat, I slid open the door and ran into the swirls. The world was like a jar of marshmallow fluff. I fell back into the wet, white, frozen precipitation and made a snow angel. Still on my back, I held the bone up to the snow. I lay palm up, cradling it as the flakes pummeled us, the gray silt of Rocky's body dripping from my fingertips into the snow as I cried.

Then it asked.

I wrapped the bone in a snowball as big as a grapefruit, packing it tight for a safe journey. I stood up, soaked, and willed that feeling through my hands as I smoothed the surface of the sphere. Then I drew my arm back, threw my shoulder forward, and launched Rocky into the comfort of the blizzard.

Drew Buxton was born in Texas in 1987 and wet the bed until the age of seven but didn't develop into a serial killer. He was Student of the Semester in 5th grade and won a coupon for a free Lu-Ann platter at Luby's. He was months away from receiving his blue belt with a black stripe down the middle in Taekwondo before he quit to pursue crippling depression and anxiety. Later he worked at Chick-Fil-A, Wendy's, and Jack in the Box, where he learned about drugs. These days he comes in at 6'2" and 235 pounds, and can tear a phonebook in half. His writing has been featured in *Vice*, *Revolver*, The *San Antonio Current*, and *Hobart*, among other publications. Find his stuff at DrewBuxton.com, or on Twitter at @droopyonalude.

....

Gerald Brennan is a self-described corporate brat who hails from the eastern half of the continent but currently resides in Chicago. He graduated from the United States Military Academy at West Point, and later earned a Master's from Columbia University's Graduate School of Journalism. He's the author of *Resistance*, *Zero Phase: Apollo 13 on the Moon*, *Project Genesis*, *Ninety-Seven to Three*, and *Public Loneliness: Yuri Gagarin's Circumlunar Flight*. He's been profiled in *Newcity*, and his writing has appeared in the *Chicago Tribune*, *The Good Men Project*, and *Innerview Magazine*. He's been a co-editor and frequent contributor at *Back to Print* and *the deadline.* More recently, he's the founder of Tortoise Books.

Follow him on Twitter at @jerry_brennan.

....

Giano Cromley was born in Montana and grew up in the shadows of the Beartooth Mountain Range. For his undergraduate studies, he went to Dartmouth College, majoring in literature and creative writing. His first port of call after college was Washington, DC, where he started off answering phones and ended up working as a speechwriter and deputy press secretary for U.S. Senator Max Baucus. But after four years of the political grind, it was time to refocus on what he'd wanted to do all along: write.

He left DC to pursue his MFA, studying fiction at the University of Montana. Three years later, it was time to hit the big city, and Chicago fit the bill. He managed to find part-time work teaching GED and ESL classes on the city's South and West Sides. Much to his surprise, he turned out to be a pretty good teacher. Eventually, he got hired to teach composition and literature at Kennedy-King College, one of the City Colleges of Chicago.

He's the author of *The Last Good Halloween* (Tortoise Books), which was a finalist for the High Plains Book Awards. His other writing - both fiction and nonfiction - has appeared in *The Threepenny Review*, *Literal Latte*, the

German edition of *Le Monde diplomatique*, *The Externalist*, *Swill Magazine*, *Word Riot*, *The Summerset Review*, *Underground Voices*, *Zouch Magazine*, and *The Bygone Bureau*. He's also been featured on the podcasts "Anything Ghost" and "WordPlaySound." In 2008, he was honored to receive an Artists Fellowship from the Illinois Arts Council. In addition, he does a variety of freelance writing projects, primarily for textbook publishers.

He lives on the South Side of Chicago with his wife and two dogs. You can follow him on Twitter at @gianoc, or via his webpage at www.gianocromley.com.

....

Darrin Doyle has lived in Saginaw, Kalamazoo, Grand Rapids, Cincinnati, Louisville, Osaka (Japan), and Manhattan (Kansas). He has worked as a paperboy, mover, janitor, telemarketer, pizza delivery driver, door-to-door salesman, copy consultant, porn store clerk, freelance writer, and technical writer, among other jobs. For a decade he played guitar in an indie rock band that made noise, recorded a couple of albums, and fell down a lot. After graduating from Western Michigan University with an MFA in fiction, he taught English in Japan for a year. He then realized he wanted to pursue fiction writing and permanently stop doing jobs he didn't love, so he earned his PhD from the University of Cincinnati.

He is the author of the novels *Revenge of the Teacher's Pet: A Love Story* (LSU Press) and *The Girl Who Ate Kalamazoo* (St. Martin's), and the short story collection *The Dark Will End the Dark* (Tortoise Books). His short stories have appeared in *Alaska Quarterly Review*, *Blackbird*, *Harpur Palate*, *Redivider*, *BULL*, and *Puerto del Sol*, among others.

Currently he teaches at Central Michigan University and lives in Mount Pleasant, Michigan with his wife and two sons. His website is www.darrindoyle.com, and you can follow him on Twitter at @DoyleDarrin.

....

Traci Failla is a fiction writer, corporate writer and blogger in Chicago whose creative work also has appeared in the Chicago Center for Literature and Photography's *The View From Here City All-Star Student Anthology* and mutterhood.com. Her blog, www.genxatmidlife.com, is supposed to chronicle the experience of middle age through the perspective of Generation X, but has turned out to be more about music than anything else. She is currently completing a novel about midlife transitions, with a heavy dose of PTA politics. Coming to fiction by way of StoryStudio, **Traci** has participated in its Novel In A Year program, Advanced Fiction

Workshops and Creative Cohort. When she's not working on her fiction, she's writing for clients on websites, blogs and industry publications, among other places. She lives with her husband, two kids and a little black cockapoo in Chicago's Lincoln Square neighborhood, fertile ground for interesting story material. You can find her on various social media sites under her name.

....

Alice Kaltman writes books for kids about surfers and mermaids and stories for adults about oddballs doing odd things. She is the author of STAGGERWING, a collection of stories forthcoming in October 2016 from Tortoise Books. Her work also appears in numerous journals including Storychord, Luna Luna Magazine, The Stockholm Review, the Atticus Review, Chicago Literati and Joyland, where her story STAY A WHILE was selected as a Longform Fiction Pick of the Week. Alice lives and surfs in Brooklyn and Montauk,

New York. Check out her website:www.alicekaltman.com for more information.

Steve Karas lives in Chicago with his wife and two kids. He is the author of *Kinda Sorta American Dream* (Tailwinds Press, 2015) and *Mesogeios* (WhiskeyPaper Press, 2016). His stories have appeared in *Necessary Fiction*, *Hobart*, *JMWW,* and elsewhere. **Steve** can be found at steve-karas.com, skaras@live.com, and @Steve_Karas.

....

Alfonso Mangione is the author of *Pottersville*, and he was a frequent contributor to *the deadline.* None of which has stopped him from being, frankly, a pretty awful human being.

....

Lily Mooney is a writer and performance artist originally from Boston. Since 2013 she's been an ensemble member of The Neo-Futurists, an experimental Chicago theater company where she has created and produced over 100 short experimental plays for the long-running late night show *Too Much Light Makes The Baby Go Blind*. She is the co-creator of *The Arrow*, a quarterly anti-storytelling event that subjects written essays to spontaneous revisions. Outside The Neo-Futurists, her short works have been produced by The Living Room Playmakers, The Chicago One-Minute Play Festival, Chicago Dramatists, and the DUMBO Arts Festival in Brooklyn. Her full-length play SMALL GAME received a production in Chicago in 2012. She has taught classes in writing and performance at The Neo-Futurists, Lake Forest College, and Northwestern University.

....

E. Yohe Moore is a public health professional living in Chicago. Her work has also appeared in *Heron Tree* and *Down* *in the Dirt.* The piece "Dry City" was inspired by summers living in Manhattan, back when the hipsters were dirtier and the trains were cheaper.

....

Joseph G. Peterson is the author of the novels *Beautiful Piece, Wanted: Elevator Man*, and *Gideon's Confession.* He has also written a book-length poem, *Inside the Whale*, and most recently a short-story collection, *Twilight of the Idiots.* He grew up in Chicago, where he works in publishing and lives with his wife and two daughters.

....

Matt Pine lives in a building with two entrances. One is in Berkeley and the other is Oakland. This offers great versatility when introducing himself. His debut novel *City Water Light & Power* was published in 2013 by Cairn Books. He reluctantly maintains a web presence at mattpine.com.

Chris Reid, longtime Chicago area slam poet, is a past winner of the Contemporary American Poetry Prize and University of Wisconsin Poetry Prize. She is a member of Big Table Writers Group and Naperville Writers Group. Her work has been published in Cram, Journal of Modern Poetry, Joy Interrupted, Midwest Review, Rhino, Rhyme and Punishment, and World Order as well as being featured on National Public Radio.

Chris holds undergraduate and graduate degrees from the University of Illinois and a certificate in Arabic Language Studies from the University of Chicago where she is a student.

Chris is employed teaching English as a Second Language to Middle Eastern refugees. She resides in suburbs with her son, Steven, who is a freshman at Illinois State University (Go Redbirds!). **Chris** is currently working on a chapbook and a stage play. When not otherwise occupied, she takes ballroom dance lessons and travels the globe.

Chris can be contacted at creid.wordsmith@gmail.com.

....

Jennifer Schaefer's work has appeared in journals such as: *North American Review*, *Chicago Tribune Printers Row*, *Curbside Splendor*, *Zouch Magazine* and *Akashic Books*' flash fiction series. She also recently received an Honorable Mention from *Glimmer Train*. In addition to writing short stories, she is seeking publication of two novels: a decadent London-based story and a YA fantasy. She lives in Evanston, Illinois, with her husband and their two daughters. You can find her at www.jenschaefer.com and on twitter @jennyschaef.

....

Originally from Los Altos, California, **Rachel Slotnick** is a painter and writer. She received her MFA from the School of the Art Institute of Chicago in May 2010. Her work is on permanent display at the Joan Flasch Artist Book Collection at the School of the Art Institute of Chicago. She is a muralist for the 35th, 46th and 47th wards, and her paintings have been displayed in a solo exhibition at Beauty & Brawn Gallery & Think Space. Recently published in *Mad Hatter's Review*, *Thrice Fiction*, and *The Brooklyn Rail*, **Rachel** was also the first place winner of Rhino Poetry's Founder's Prize, and nominated for the Pushcart Prize in 2015. **Rachel** currently resides in Chicago where she works as Adjunct Faculty in Art Studio and English at Malcolm X College, the School of the Art Institute of Chicago, and the Illinois Art Institute, and the School of the Art Institute of Chicago.

She's the author of the poetry collection *In Lieu Of Flowers* (Tortoise Books). See the full scope of her work at www.rachelslotnick.com or follow her on Twitter at @rlslotnick.

....

Ben Tanzer is the author of the books *My Father's House*, *You Can Make Him Like You*, *So Different Now*, *Orphans*, *Lost in Space: A Father's Journey There and Back Again*, *The New York Stories*, and the upcoming memoir *Be Cool*. **Ben** serves as Director of Publicity and Content Strategy at Curbside Splendor Publishing and can be found online at *This Blog Will Change Your Life*, the center of his growing lifestyle empire. He lives in Chicago with his wife and two sons.

ABOUT TORTOISE BOOKS

Slow and steady wins in the end, but the book industry often focuses on the fast-seller. Tortoise Books is dedicated to finding and promoting quality authors who haven't yet found a niche in the marketplace—writers producing memorable and engaging works that will stand the test of time.

http://www.tortoisebooks.com/

Printed in the USA
CPSIA information can be obtained
at www.ICGtesting.com
JSHW022216140824
68134JS00018B/1080